DEATH
ADJACENT

BY JESSICA MATHEWS

ISBN-13: 978-1984013910

LCCN: 2018901092

Cover art designed by Jennifer Stolzer of Jennifer Stolzer Illustrations using graphics from shutterstock.com contributed by artists: Jose Ignacio Soto, tsuneomp, and tatui suwat

To all those I have loved and lost

along the way

Bekka & Sherry,

What will you do with your eternity?

Jessica Mas

Chapter 1

My story begins and ends in the same place, though I'm none too happy about it. Just once when I die I'd like to stay dead. Thoughts of my afterlife left my body making room for the new breaths I needed to take to kick start my consciousness and vital organs again. My eyes popped open on the third exhale.

Damn. Where was I this time?

Ice pressed against my spine, a combination of the stainless steel table I laid on and a sub-zero room temperature suffocating the paper-thin sheet that pretended to cover me. I drifted in and out of consciousness only semi-aware of what was happening to my body. I spent my conscious moments willing my limbs to move rather unsuccessfully. The intermingling smells of decay and military-grade disinfectant felt like fire being forced down my throat. My eyes burned from the causticity making them water until they were wide with horror at the sick realization of what was happening to me. Tears screamed down my cheeks in two white hot lines marring my complexion. A figure, still a shadow to my blurry eyes, didn't notice my tears or my pain at waking up alive yet again. It moved above me, going about its business, not caring that I existed below.

Since the first time I died I've only existed in the below, the in between of life and death. These were the kind of shadows the living stay out of if they want to continue living, the same shadows the things that hate the light avoid because they know I exist there. And that I am hunting them.

My body was still paralyzed and my pulse no longer barely palpable. My heartbeat was getting stronger. Blood rushed to my ears in an attempt to deafen me. My anxiety rose in my chest to help my heartbeat undo all of the work I had just done in an effort to leave this place.

The shadow was so close I heard its heart pulsating to the rhythms of the job it was rendering. Cologne and sweat were strong enough to catch in my throat. A familiar faint red tinge slowly creeped up my neck towards my face.

I was naked. Shit. Took me long enough to figure that out. This was the slowest I had ever come back from a death. However I died must have been bad if it was taking this long for me to come back. A whiff of cologne brought me back to being naked. Why was I naked? Where was I? What was this guy doing to me?

Being naked is so unmistakable you would know it even if you were dead. It's also embarrassing as hell. Especially if you're a carb-loving woman of traditional Italian descent like me. It's the one thing I don't do even when I'm alone. When your body is nothing but a freak show of lumpy body parts and thin white cellulite lines racing thick pink scars all over the surface of your skin, you don't jump at the opportunity to show people what's under your clothes. There aren't many people jumping at the chance to take a peek either. Who was this guy and what did he want from me? When I could move again there would be hell to pay for sure.

My eyes cleared. I no longer had the cataract of death clouding my sight. Or my judgment.

A man in scrubs and too many layers of plastic protective gear lurched over me like Dr. Frankenstein on a good night, knife in one surgically gloved hand, muttering to himself (probably about which body part he needed to take from me to complete his arson-phobic monster). A gloved hand, resolute in its obligation to its master, brushed my right shoulder. I could feel the warmth emanating from the man's body through the sheer layer of latex that kept our skin from

3

touching. Through the warmth, I sensed this man was cold, calculating even, when it came to performing his duty.

He pinned me down, pressing my back further against the stainless steel table using little force or effort. He didn't have to exert much power or energy in my direction. I wasn't going anywhere and he knew it. He expected me to comply because no one had resisted him before. I didn't complain. I couldn't. I couldn't cry out, scream or run. I didn't panic until I felt the blade he held slice open my skin with vigor and precision. Three swift strokes wielded by a deft hand

This was his job and he was good at it. Judging by his thinning gray hair and the wrinkles around his dead eyes, this had been his job for twenty some-odd years before I graced his table. It would probably be his job for another twenty some-odd years after me if his overweight body didn't give out first.

I finally realized what was happening. Give me a break, people! This was my first autopsy.

The medical examiner had done this so many times before he didn't even have to look at me to know where to cut. Or maybe dead people didn't normally complain if his lines weren't exactly even.

Great, more scars to add to my growing collection.

Usually, when I die, I wake up in whatever dark hole I had just spent the night sending a demon slinking back to. This was the first time I'd woken up in a morgue being treated like a proper dead person. This was also the first time I couldn't remember how I died.

That old adage about there being a first time for everything was really sticking in my craw here. For those of you who aren't southerners like I am, what I mean to say is that I was getting really pissed off. Don't worry, being a little pissed off and a little hungry all the time was my normal temperature. If you ever meet me in person you'd figure that out pretty quick.

Now that I was properly motivated by anger, I had to get up and take care of some business. No longer able to play the part of the corpse in this sick charade, I willed my limbs to move. My body was healing rapidly and just returning to normal. The Y incision the doctor had so carefully made to open my chest became a crude V shape. The medical examiner's face switched from bored rote memory to utter shock when he saw my lackluster performance as a stiff.

He clutched his chest, smearing my blood on his white lab coat with his right hand. He was sweating so much his light blue dress shirt was soaked through, which was a feat in and of itself since the room we were in was only about fifty-five degrees below zero. I guess I was the freshest corpse he had ever seen. His face turned beet red (which I resented because *I* was the one who was *naked* in front of a stranger). He licked his lips and gasped for air.

My eyes followed his name tag swinging back and forth in front of my face, briefly hypnotizing me. Dr. Albert Morton, Southern Provincial Hospital. I was back in town? I vaguely remembered being in the city doing… something. Getting into trouble apparently. How did I get here? Why couldn't I remember anything from last night? I usually remembered.

Was it even still last night or had I actually been dead for a lot longer than I thought? How long can someone be dead before they just couldn't come back from it at all? Was this an alternate death reality? This sure as shit wasn't heaven. It didn't seem all that hellish either. I'd been through worse than freezing my tits off during an autopsy. Not remembering what happened to me was actually worse than surviving my first autopsy. Maybe I didn't want my story to end with an autopsy after all. Especially if there was a chance I might survive it.

I came out of my reverie in time to watch the good doctor fall to the tiled floor. I heard his body crack as he landed on the cream-colored tiles. His limp body covered the drain stopping my blood from being washed away. I felt almost relieved by the fact that I couldn't be thrown away so easily.

I have to admit I almost left him on the floor. I mean here I was struggling to live through my *autopsy* and this joker was the one who was havin' a freakin' heart attack! Just what I needed, me naked, bleeding and having to perform CPR on this guy so I wouldn't feel like the shittiest person alive for letting him die. I probably shouldn't have done CPR on the guy. I wasn't too sure I was doing it right. I hadn't been certified in years. I fell into it pretty easy though. I think it's just like what people say about riding a bike. You never forget. I mean I'm pretty sure what I was doing to the medical examiner was CPR. Like I said though, it had been a while.

Of course, the medical examiner's assistant had to walk in on the most awkward version of the tango known to man. My boobs were bouncing erratically as I pummeled the heavy-set man's chest. The medical examiner's assistant just stood there mouth gaping like he had never seen a corpse perform CPR. Well, I guess he hadn't or I wouldn't be the only undead unknown in town.

To my knowledge there was no one else that existed like me. It was sometimes a lonely feeling. I mean, would I outlive everyone I knew and loved? Or did I have a certain number of deaths like a cat? I didn't know my exact number. I know in the past year I had died more than nine times so I was guessing I wasn't infused with feline blood.

"I'm Mitch. I'm your biggest fan. *Asylum's Assassin* is my favorite comic book of all time." The assistant stepped closer holding out his hand.

Oh, great, a fanboy. Just what I always wanted. "I don't know what you're talking about, kid." I turned away from the assistant and back to the dying guy I was starting to get tired of trying to save. "Give me your lab coat." I turned back to the assistant as an afterthought. Despite the exercise I was letting my body suffer through at the moment, my core body temperature was not increasing. I was still freezing and uncomfortable.

The assistant looked about twelve years old. He had a sweet half-cocked smile that showed off a dimple on one side. His blond hair was styled in a beach bum wave. There weren't any beaches around here for hundreds of miles. The kid was out of place in a big way. My senses were starting to come back to me. Something wasn't right here. Something about Mitch was so very *off*. I struggled to remember any of the training I had gone through after my first death.

I stopped doing CPR on the medical examiner. I hadn't gotten a pulse yet and it had been too long. Even if I were able to revive him now he would have significant brain damage. I knew his death wasn't entirely my fault. That didn't change things. I was tired of losing humans on my watch. Demons I didn't mind losing so much.

Mitch was no boy scout. Hell, Mitch wasn't even human. Just the way I liked my men- evil and about to die. My training kicked back in. I registered the stench of Sulphur rolling off Mitch with enough abundance to make me gag. I caught the red glint in his irises before they went back to brown. I'm sure the real Mitch was a sweet kid. Now, his body was filled to the brim with demon spawn. Not for long.

"Mitch was it?" I stepped backward over the medical examiner's corpse. There was a set of instruments he had used on me to perform my autopsy that would come in handy when this whole thing with my 'biggest fan' went sour in a big way.

"Don't worry, Selene, I won't tell anyone. No one will even know you were here." Mitch dropped the cute act forming a smile on his face I knew contained some version of evil I couldn't be bothered with right now.

I really didn't have time for this shit. Did I mention I was still naked and still not close enough to the medical instruments to grab one?

"So you know how I got here? The last thing I remember, I was in the city dancing." My eyes darted from Mitch to the autopsy table and back again. I was crouched low ready to sprint to the table. There was too much distance between me and the table and not enough between me and Mitch.

Mitch followed my gaze and laughed. "My master brought you here. You've been known to cheat death. I was assigned to finish the job." Mitch didn't lunge at me like I thought he would. Instead, he went for the only thing in this room either one of us could use as a weapon.

He threw a scalpel at me. I stood to let it hit me in the shoulder. It hurt like a son of a bitch. At least I had a weapon now. My shoulder only bled a little before the wound closed up. I had a feeling this was going to be one of those wounds that hurts more during cold snaps than they do when you first come by them. Oh, well, I'll just add it to my growing collection.

I twirled the scalpel in my right hand and shrugged. It was now or never. I charged demon Mitch dodging the rest of the medical equipment Mitch decided to throw.

"Jesus, Selene! Why is it every time I see you you're either naked or killing someone?"

I was thisclose to stabbing Mitch in the eye with my scalpel when a familiar voice interrupted us causing us to both turn toward the sound. A portly man in a tan sheriff uniform ran his left hand through his thinning hair unable to smooth out the grimace that contorted his face. I shrugged in response and used my left hand to push Mitch's cheek away from me. I figured Mitch would look fashion forward in a Columbian necktie. I readied my right hand tightening my grip on the scalpel.

"Give me a minute, Sheriff. Mitch and I have to conclude our business." I turned back to Mitch.

He dodged my scalpel to the throat maneuver.

"Come on, man, my ride back to Vampireville is here." I swiped the scalpel in Mitch's general direction again. He was too fast for my just-back-from-the-dead reflexes. The scalpel cut the air in front of me and nothing else.

"Selene, you know how everyone hates when you call Asylum 'Vampireville.'" I could hear the sheriff talking, I wasn't looking in his direction. He was somewhere behind me probably fidgeting like a squirrel with a nut.

I was trying to focus on Mitch. The same Mitch who pretended to be a medical examiner's assistant just to make sure I didn't come back from the dead. The same Mitch that was a demon disguised as a human. The same Mitch whose disguise wasn't even that good but I had let it slide because I had just woken up during my autopsy. I shouldn't have let it slide. Now, I was going to slide this blade down Mitch's throat.

"Come on, Selene, I heard you were better than this." Mitch bobbed up and down on the balls of his feet, taunting me.

I hated it when the demon I was hunting had worse ADHD than me. I needed this kid to be still for five seconds so I could kill him. This death had been harder on me than any other I had experienced since the first time I died. I wasn't bouncing back like I normally did. I wanted to know why. The more pressing matter was the demon blocking my view of Larry by stretching his arms as wide as they would go.

I didn't need an easier target than the one in front of me. I vaulted toward Mitch letting the scalpel move where it willed. Mitch laughed and jumped out of the way. This super-speed shit was getting old. The scalpel sliced open part of Mitch's shirt revealing part of a tattoo. A tattoo I had seen before.

I stopped cold as the memory of the last time I had seen that tattoo washed panic over my entire being. I couldn't see the woman clearly. Her black hair stood out because her short hair was cut into a bob and was topped with a crown that looked like a striking snake. The woman's face was blurry. I felt like I knew she would not be kind if she caught me staring at her. Like I had met her before and just

9

couldn't place her. On her right wrist, under several bangle bracelets, was the same tattoo Mitch had. I recognized the Eye of Horus from a history class I had taken once. This eye was not traditionally drawn. This eye was closed in open defiance of everything Horus stood for.

Somewhere in the distance I heard shouting and two loud noises that sounded like gunshots. I had pain in my abdomen that came on too fast to stop. I took a few gulping breaths as I looked up. Mitch was lying on the floor. Or rather, his clothes were lying on the floor shrouding a pile of charcoal colored ash. Sheriff Larry Baker was standing over the clothed ash pile holding his service revolver. Darn. I wanted to be the one to kill a demon today. The thought that someone should sweep up what was left of Mitch crossed my mind. I imagined Larry getting a broom and sweeping Mitch into a dust pan. I may have giggled at that point. I'm not sure. I was well on my way to dying again.

"Dammit, Selene!" Larry cursed loud enough to create an echo in the mostly empty room that deafened me.

I winced from the noise. "What happened?" I was totally yelling. Larry must have fired the gun at close range to me. I couldn't tell if one of my eardrums had burst or not. The pain in my abdomen dictated all thoughts at the moment.

Larry caught me as I fell to the floor. "I'm sorry I shot you, Selene. One of the bullets that hit that demon must have been a through and through."

Larry grabbed the sheet that had covered me earlier during my autopsy and covered me with it again. I could hear Larry swear. I smiled. Some of the made up cuss words he was saying now were things he taught me a few months ago when we were trapped in the back of a semi-truck headed south to be sold on the black market. We had a lot of fun killing folk that night.

My head was spinning. I had lost too much blood to keep my eyes open. Larry must have hit something vital. Some parts of the body take longer to regenerate than others. "Larry," I grabbed the collar of his standard issue sheriff uniform and pulled his ear closer to my mouth. "I remembered," I whispered before dying. Again.

Chapter 2

I sat up in bed, sucking in all of the air I could fill my lungs with. I felt like a fish drowning on land. I couldn't get enough oxygen inside of me. I would have started using my arms to scoop the air into me if I hadn't felt like I wasn't alone and if that wouldn't have been weird.

"You're alright, Selene." Sheriff Larry was sitting beside my bed reading the local newspaper, *The Daily Cud*, not even looking in my direction.

How could he know if I was alright or not if he wasn't even paying attention to me?

I'd always hated the name of the town's newspaper. I thought it was stupid to name a newspaper after cud, which was something that cows chewed all day long. I tried to tell that to the paper's editor a few years ago. *The Cud* was a town tradition dating back a few hundred years give or take. Geoffrey was taking no part in hearing how much I hated the name of a beloved tradition. The sleepy town of Hereford was located so far south in the great state of Tennessee that you could practically spit on the Alabama border. Their chief trade was cattle, anything to do with cattle- husbandry, dairy, rodeo, whatever. If you name it and it is something you can do to a cow, a cow can do to you or a cow can do for themselves we do it here in Hereford. That's why the town's paper was named after the crap the cow keeps in his mouth all day. I mean, I guess it could have been named after something the cow does on the other end so we've got that going for us.

"Chewing anything good today, Larry?" I laughed a little at my joke.

Larry didn't even crack a smile. Probably because I made that joke a lot. I know I'm really not all that funny. Knowing that kind of makes me want to tell jokes more. Must be something stubborn in my personality.

"Your wound healed up nice. Sorry I killed you again. I know how much you hate that." To his credit, I'm pretty sure Larry was actually sincere in his apology.

Even before he was infected with lycanthropy he had pledged his life, first as sheriff's deputy then as sheriff, to helping and protecting the people of this town. Me included. Now that he was a werewolf, he joined a pack of other werewolves that make it their mission to protect and serve any and all humans. I'm not included in that because I'm not exactly human. I've saved all of their butts so many times though, they owe me.

"It's cool, Lar. I feel like I needed a re-set anyway. Something wasn't right the last time I came back." I sat up in bed smoothing out the duvet around me.

Larry picked up his coffee mug and frowned. It must have been empty. He got up and handed me *The Cud*. "Check out the front page." Larry left, presumably in search of more caffeine to feed his addiction.

I unfurled the newspaper smoothing out the creases in the front page. I was not thrilled with the headline.

County Medical Examiner Needs Autopsy

13

Harrumph, I'd lived around some of the morons who ran the paper for as long as I could remember. None of them were ever all that creative. I guess they thought a coroner needing an autopsy was funny. I didn't and I'd be the first person to laugh at a bad pun. And I would laugh hard. If I was working at the paper which, as a new bylaw in the town charter, I wasn't allowed to, I would use the headline "Death Examines Coroner" or something like that. Well, anyway, I already told you I wasn't funny or allowed anywhere within a mile radius of the newspaper building. Maybe I would work there if I hadn't died last year.

That was sort of the reason why I wasn't allowed near the building anymore. I died right in it. Then, started a small fire. A small fire that turned into a larger fire pretty quick. Whatever. It was that vampire's fault I reflexively kicked over a lantern in the throes of death anyway. If he hadn't of snatched me during a hayride and drug me into the nearest building (which just so happened to be the newspaper offices), I wouldn't have been carrying a portable kerosene lantern and if he hadn't killed me I never would have kicked said lantern into a pile of archived newspapers. At any rate, a lot of the building caught fire faster than anyone ever thought it could. Good news (Get it- news? Fine! I'll just go be funny over here. By myself.) Good news was that the newspaper got a new and better building in the center of town.

The center of town also happened to be where Asylum was located. I live in Asylum so every day I break the restraining order Judge Donnelson issued that stated I was to go no more than a mile near the newspaper or The Cud's staff. My boss, James, says I got off easy. I could have been charged with arson and sent to the women's prison in the city.

Even though it wasn't my fault.

When I died last year, I was brought to Vampireville, I mean, Asylum, to see if I would turn into a vampire from the bite that killed me. I never did. I just woke up healed like nothing had ever happened. The Covenant is the governing body who rule over all supernatural creatures. Asylum is their underground network that is charged with locating all supernatural creatures. Asylum can help or hurt depending on how you became what you were and if you follow the rules of the Covenant or not.

They didn't give me such a choice. I am Asylum's chief monster hunter. I think mostly because so far every time I've died I've come back to life. James, the vampire in charge of this Asylum, basically told me that I was to do this job for him or be put to death. I told him to shove death up his ass because it was apparent to both of us that I couldn't die. He said he didn't say it would be a quick death and I should choose wisely.

I chose quick death. Hopefully, a demon or some other nasty bump in the night gets lucky and kills me one day in a way where I actually stay dead. It would be a nice change of pace for me.

When you know you can't die, you don't fear death. When you know you can't die and sometimes wish you could, you don't fear anything. You welcome the afterlife with open arms and a genuine smile on your face. Although, I have died so many times maybe this was my afterlife. If what I was in right now was my afterlife maybe I should ask for a refund. I was living in a town filled with humans who couldn't stop reminding me about the parts of my life I would rather forget. It really wasn't my idea of a good time. It briefly dawned on me that maybe given what I'd done in this life warranted me a shitty afterlife. I didn't deserve to ask for a refund. I wanted one nonetheless.

I looked down. I was picking at a long scar on my right forearm. I had no idea how I got the scar but I'd had it for longer than I had been undead. I tended to play with it when I was thinking. Thinking required more than playing with a cut that smoothed over my skin long ago. Caffeine sounded good at the moment. So did any type of breakfast meat the Asylum cafeteria could offer. I took a few minutes to shower and put on clothes before wandering downstairs to the cafeteria.

Asylum was built underground directly under the courthouse in the town square. The cavern it was built in was designed so that you thought you were in some kind of antebellum manor house in the ritzy part of the nearest city with a population of more than a thousand. Behind all of the wood paneling that lined the halls I knew there was nothing but solid rock. Granite I think. That made tunneling out hard to do. Not that I've tried. If I had, I wouldn't have been the first one to try.

I was in the residential section. I had a suite which meant no kitchen. I did get two bedrooms and my own full bathroom out of this whole living in a monster hotel deal. It also meant I was on the top floor which to me meant I was that much closer to the surface and my freedom. You never realize how much you miss fresh air and sunshine when your job is done mostly at night and during the day you're persona non grata in town and have to spend most of your time underground. Literally underground. Like the townsfolk didn't already walk all over me when I did make the rare appearance topside. Sometimes I wonder why I bother saving them in the first place. Then, I think of people like Dr. Morton who didn't deserve to die because of something I did or didn't do.

So, I live in Asylum and I help the helpless. I take in stray werewolves and train them to control their urges, to control their shifts, to stop them from becoming a mindless animal, to keep some part of their human self when they turn so they don't go on a rampage and kill everyone from here to the Bama border. I kill rogue demons and vampires who can't or won't follow the rules. I find creatures nature created then threw away like garbage and I do my best to care for them and love them.

Like Reginald. He was a griffin. Albeit a thousand year old griffin who always looks like he's about to croak at any minute but a griffin nonetheless. Griffins are said to protect priceless treasure. To Reggie, knowledge was the most priceless treasure. So, I got him a job in the Asylum library after I found him chained up in an old bootlegger's cave on a routine mission to kill some rogue vamps. I guess he tasted better than he looked otherwise he would have been dead long before I found him. He never told me what happened to him or how long he had been there. The only thing Reggie ever told me about that night was that he was glad I was the one who saved him.

The library was down the two flights of steps and to the right from my room. It was also on the way to the cafeteria which was down another flight of stairs past the library. I decided to ask Reggie to research the tattoo that had stopped me cold during my fight with Mitch earlier. It would give him something to do and me the chance to consume more breakfast meats than should have been possible for a girl my size before I actually had to do any work today.

I opened one of the doors to the enormous library the Covenant somehow managed to cram underground with the rest of the weirdos and decrepit monsters. There were couches and chairs scattered about on top of oriental rugs, some writing desks, a lot of lamps and the walls were covered in floor to ceiling bookshelves. You know the kind that have those crazy ladders attached to them so you can get something off the very top shelf and touch the ceiling at the same time? Yeah, that's what I was looking at.

When I looked up I was blinded by a chandelier so large it took up most of the room. It was a good thing the ceiling was so high or even I would have hit my head on it when I walked in which would have been a feat. I think I mentioned how short I was before? Five foot nothing is miniscule compared to everyone else in the world and I'm including fourth graders.

"Mistress Selene, good to see you up and about." Reginald bowed as low as he could without falling over. His thinning grey hair was neatly combed to compliment the three piece suit he always wore. Today his vest was purple with gold filigree. It looked good on him.

"Reggie, my man, good to see *you* up and about." I clapped him on the back lightly. I didn't want to be the reason he broke a hip.

"I surmise you want something unless you are hiding from Master James." Reggie turned from me to frown at a book older than him before shelving it on a wheeled cart.

"A little of both actually." I shrugged my shoulders at his back like I would have if he hadn't turned away from me.

Reggie sighed and put the book he was holding back on a low shelf. He straightened up. Waiting. Reggie was always waiting for someone to tell him what to do. I didn't have the patience or the willpower to wait like that. I also hated being told what to do.

I drew the closed Eye of Horus the best I could on a scrap of paper I found on Reggie's desk and handed it to him. "I need to know everything you do about this symbol. I remembered seeing it before. I didn't remember the context. It's driving me crazy."

Reggie startled, dropping the scrap of paper I handed him. He stooped down to pick up the paper faster than I ever could before righting himself again. "The Eye of Horus is a symbol meant to protect royalty. It is open to show Horus himself is always watching. This eye is closed. This is an aberration. I cannot help you."

Reggie tried to press the paper back into my hands. I didn't take it. Instead, the scrap floated toward the floor. Neither Reggie nor I bent to pick it up. When the scrap of paper settled itself on the hardwood floor between us we both looked up from watching the paper fall.

"Can't help me or won't?" I didn't raise my voice above a whisper. I knew Reggie could hear me.

"Mistress," Reggie sighed, folding his body in on itself making himself as small as possible. This action caused his shirt to pull out of his trousers in the back and wrinkle his jacket creating a disheveled look he had never shown before.

Whatever this symbol was, it was spooking an unshakable magical being to his very core.

Reggie shook himself upright. As he smoothed out his clothes a mist formed around him. He used his magic to transform from a frail elderly man into a creature with the body of a lion, the head and wings of a great eagle and a serpent for a tail.

I didn't need to feel his paws crushing my chest or his tail wrapped around my throat to know in griffin form Reggie was a force to be reckoned with. Maybe I had taken our conversation too far? Reggie was a guy I didn't relish fighting. Ever.

The griffin in front of me still had Reggie's voice which was always disconcerting to me since Reggie rarely, if ever, changed forms in public. He was taller than I was now which wasn't really something to write home about since he would have been taller than me in his man form had his spine not been so stooped.

Reggie stared down at me from his now intimidating height. "Mistress, this is a symbol I have not seen in an age. This is the calling card of a mad woman and a sign of terrible things to come."

"Wha-?" I didn't have time to ask Reggie what he meant before I was flying through the air. I almost hurled. If I was meant to fly, I would have been born with wings.

Reggie used his lion paws to clutch my body to his chest while he used the cavernous library to his advantage. He flew across the expanse of the library to a tunnel on the far end. The few people in the library startled when Reggie flew overhead. I guess he had never stretched his wings like this before.

Reggie touched down mid-way through the tunnel and set me down. I immediately fell to the ground. I was not meant to fly, especially unexpectedly. My whole body was shaking. I rolled onto my stomach preparing to vomit. I heaved. Nothing came out. Reggie was still in griffin form. He used his tail to right my body and hold me up against the stone wall. I don't know how long it took for my body to stop shaking until I finally felt like I was no longer standing on a paint mixer that someone had left on all night.

When I could stand on my own, Reggie transformed back into his human form. He drew a silver key ring out of his pocket that held, maybe four or five keys. One key in particular caught my eye. The head of the key was shaped like a gold scarab with some kind of writing down its back. I blinked as hard as I could. My brain was trying to remember something it just couldn't. I knew I had seen that scarab before. A part of me felt like I could read the writing even though it was written in another language and I barely spoke English.

Reggie felt along the stone tunnel wall until he found what he was looking for. He used the scarab key to unlock a door I hadn't known was there. I didn't know what I expected to happen when I walked through a secret door at Vampireville. I certainly didn't expect *nothing* to happen. The whole situation seemed like it should have been much cooler than that. I was kind of disappointed I didn't end up in another world or walk in on a group of elderly werewolves doing water aerobics or something.

Reggie chuckled behind me. I'd never heard him laugh before.

"What's so funny?" I spun around to face him pulling my hands to my hips.

"Mistress, your imagination is quite overactive. I could feel the disappointment leeching off of you after you walked over the threshold." Reggie finished locking the secret door behind us and started walking up a flight of stone steps lit only with torches on wall sconces every few feet or so. The torches were lit before we walked in so someone had to constantly patrol this hallway just to keep the home fires blazing.

I felt like a princess being taken to a tall tower in a land far, far away. I didn't have any choice except to follow Reggie and see where his sudden onset madness led us.

I got up the first flight of stairs no problem. When we started to ascend the second flight my body protested. I leaned my forehead against the stone wall soaking up the coolness of stones that had been underground for longer than I had been alive. I should have been thoroughly embarrassed that Reggie was outpacing me without eking out so much as one drop of sweat. I didn't have the energy to be angry at the moment and I knew I would never change. I hated exercise and loved booze too much for that. I took a deep breath and willed my body from its resting position to continue the climb.

Reggie was waiting for me about five steps up around a corner on a landing. If I would have known that a few minutes ago, I still would have stopped where I did to catch my breath. He pulled the scarab key out of his waistcoat pocket again. Another twinge of remembrance coursed through my body, the moment too fleeting to grasp any true memory. Reggie went into the room and lit a lantern with a book of matches from a table by the door. He hung the lantern from a hook hanging in the center of the little room. That one simple action caused the entire room to light up. Lantern light bounced off several well placed mirrors cascading light all around me.

The room was so bright I had to close my eyes. I re-opened my eyes deliberately. Once they adjusted, I was able to see why we were here. The room was filled with wine racks on every wall. Instead of wine, each holder had a scroll of parchment. There was a small bookshelf slightly taller than me that held leather bound journals. Reggie knew about this place because it was an extension of the library. I guess when you're immortal you keep your special things in secret dungeons. Too bad there wasn't any wine down here. I could have used some right about now.

Reggie was on the far side of the room pulling scroll after scroll from a row, unfurling them, then frowning and muttering under his breath. I had no idea what he was looking for so I sat down at the table in the center of the room and waited for him to tell me. Reggie found what he was looking for. He laid the scroll on the table in front of me.

"The last time this marking was seen, Cleopatra, Pharaoh of Egypt, tried to start a revolution against Octavian to keep him from taking control over her lands. That was over two thousand years ago." Reggie unfurled the scroll as he told me the story of the closed Eye of Horus.

I watched as Reggie's voice caused the hieroglyphs to dance around the parchment.

"Cleopatra had twin children, a boy and a girl, named Alexander and Selene. When her daughter came of age, Selene was to marry Alexander and follow him to the throne. Legend says she threw away her chance at the throne for the love of a soldier and those events led to both her death and new life among the immortals."

Reggie was still talking. I couldn't hear anything except my own heart beating its way out of my body. My chest constricted with panic. I couldn't be in this dungeon anymore. The memories were overwhelming. I stood up to leave. I didn't make it far before all of the things I had been trying to remember flooded back into my consciousness taking me to another time.

~

I looked at the woman standing before me. She was wearing a flowy gold dress and more jewels than there were in the whole British Empire. Her hair was a jet black bob. She wore her eyeliner like a boss and a diadem shaped like a striking snake which told me she actually was the boss. She was also my mom and she was pissed.

"Selene, we have been over this and over this. You must marry Alexander if you are to take the throne. You are the oldest even though it is only by three minutes. The throne is your birthright. However, you need Alexander to rule with you. I will not let you marry beneath your station. We must keep the royal bloodlines pure." My mother frowned at my decision to not marry my twin brother so we could sit on her throne together. She pushed the bangles on her right wrist around revealing a closed Eye of Horus tattoo.

"I don't even want to rule. Give the throne to Alexander. I'm not marrying him." I was shouting back at her. I was a teenager. I didn't want to rule. I didn't want to get married. I didn't want the life my mother had chosen for us. It wouldn't matter much anyway. Octavian's armies would be coming for us soon to change our fates without our permission.

~

I woke up on the floor of the library dungeon with Reggie standing over me fanning my face with one of the leather bound journals.

I bolted upright. "I'm Cleopatra's daughter? Like, THE CLEOPATRA? Pharaoh of Egypt?"

Reggie frowned. "If you are Cleopatra's daughter and the legends about her are true, that would explain your regenerative capabilities more than your recent vampire bite. I'm afraid I would have to research this more to be able to tell you for certain. If you are two thousand years old, where have you been all this time? What have you been doing?"

"I-I don't know." All of the excitement that had welled up inside of me after remembering who I was deflated like the air in my lungs.

Reggie was right. If I were immortal, shouldn't I be able to remember at least the last century of my life? If I wasn't Cleopatra's daughter though, who was I and why was I having memories only she would have?

Chapter 3

I left Reggie in the secret room filled with ancient texts. I couldn't stay in there anymore. I had a sudden itch to kill something. Being still and doing research wasn't something I liked anyway. That's what I had Reggie for. It didn't matter what he found. I was ninety-nine percent positive that I was Cleopatra's daughter. I doubted if we were distant cousins or something that I would be having her memories. We also had the same name. If that didn't cement my birthright then I didn't know what else would.

The tunnel Reggie had flown me to earlier was clear when I cracked the door at the bottom of the stairs. I stepped out of the secret door and pulled it closed behind me. I felt along the stone wall. I couldn't find the seams of the door and I was standing right in front of it. I shook my head. Magic was cool to an extent, though it usually just ended up pissing me off. I turned left from the door to continue down the tunnel away from the library. I knew this tunnel would eventually lead me out topside. I walked up the tunnel's incline until I slipped out of Asylum at the side of the courthouse. Sunset was setting in making it easier for me to go unseen. I had an hour or so before it would be full dark. I walked around to the front of the courthouse. My plan was to take Main Street to Seventh so I could hit up a local bar that catered to my particular crowd. Even though I didn't have the bad looks of a ghoul, I still didn't hang around with the locals. Many of them were pissed at me for various reasons and I don't deal in angry humans.

I was going to have to deal with some riff-raff before I could get a much needed drink. When I rounded the corner, I saw a small group of bikers hanging out in the handicap parking spaces near the front of the courthouse. They were laughing and drinking beer. A lot of beer judging by the amount of crumpled blue and silver cans at their feet. A lot of beer and a lot of blood. There was a dead man lying at the feet of the vampires being slowly buried in beer cans. The man looked homeless. Made sense as to why no one reported this to Asylum. No one was missing this guy. Where the hell were the patrols though? How long had these guys been allowed to stand here flagrantly flouting all of the rules while standing on top of Asylum? I'd have to rip someone a new one later. Now, I had to take care of business.

The vampires' leather biker jackets said *Fang Army*. Their fangs said "you look delicious please let me put your neck in my mouth." Entitled bastards. I really hated vampires most of the time which sucked for me since I worked for one.

The biggest vampire out of the bunch must have had the most to drink. He taunted me and tried to grab my arm. The other five egged him on, provoking him to take a drink and pass me around. Didn't they know who they were dealing with?

"You guys don't want me. I have blood cancer. I will taste horrible." I tried to back up. I couldn't. They were circling me. I hoped I wasn't about to get my ass handed to me by five vampires who didn't give a shit about the consequences Asylum handed out for draining humans. Okay, so I wasn't human, but still. The odds were against me here. I never know when to mind my own damn business or call for back up.

"You wouldn't believe how many times I've heard that line from someone I was about to bleed dry. Any last words or wishes, sweetheart?" The big guy pulled me closer by my right wrist.

Another vampire, a skinny one with shoulder length blonde hair, said through his teeth, "We are nothing if not southern gentlemen." Then, he spit blood all over the faces of the two guys to his left before he turned to ash at their feet.

They didn't know who I was. I didn't recognize them which meant they were probably just passing thorough. Too bad I wasn't going to leave them alive long enough to ask. I held up the silver stake I had used on the "southern gentleman" vampire. The big guy didn't let my wrist go. He held me out away from his body so the rest of his crew could finish me off and so I couldn't reach him to drive the stake through his heart.

Didn't matter. My odds were looking up. One down, four to go.

"See what I can do? I told you drinking my blood would kill you. You should have listened." I tucked my knees to my chest in as tight of a ball as I could manage. Then, I kicked my legs out making contact with the lead vampire's chest.

He wasn't bothered by my kick so much as he was by my surmised insolence. The vampire threw me against the row of motorcycles.

Ugh, that was going to leave a mark. I struggled to breathe through what I was pretty sure were cracked if not broken ribs. I leaned on the motorcycle to steady myself as I got up. The motorcycle must have been at a tipping point. When I put all of my weight on it, the motorcycle went down taking out all of the other motorcycles in the row like dominos.

The immensely muscular vampire was beyond pissed now. Vampire or not, you don't mess with bikers' rides. He sniffed the air all around him tasting something none of us could see. "Wolves, scatter boys!"

Wolves? Where? I scanned the distance. Nothing. I sniffed my shirt. I had just showered and I hadn't been training any new wolves lately. Where was this guy getting the scent of wolves from?

Didn't matter. The four remaining vampires, including the giant they called their leader, made their way toward their motorcycles, toward me. Shit. I had lost my stake either mid-air or during my fall. I broke off a side mirror from the nearest motorcycle then went to work. I couldn't let these guys get away if for nothing else except to bolster my pride though, to be fair, I did find them sucking in the worst way. I would probably be saving a ton of human lives if I dusted these guys.

I ran toward the closest vamp, a scrawny guy who couldn't have been more than a teenager when he was turned, waiting until I got close before I ducked under his outstretched arms jabbing at his rib cage with the sharp end of the broken mirror. The teenage vampire dusted itself all over my jacket. While the ashes of the former human would come out well enough, the smell of Sulphur would never leave. I would have to live with it or burn this jacket. We all know later I would burn the jacket the first chance I got. Sulphur was not a smell I could live with or something my over-worked dry cleaner would be able to get out of this jacket.

For those of you keeping score at home, the only living (eh, semi-living) things still standing in front of the courthouse were me and three vampire bikers who were seriously driving me up a wall. The leader and one of the other vampires got their motorcycles off the ground and started while I was picking off the third vampire- another scrawny teenager.

What was with this weirdo? Did he think teenagers were easy to handle? All of the teens I've ever met were broodier than vampires and never did what they were told. The vampire went down in a blur of ashes and shrieks of terror. I had caught him from behind, jabbed one of his kidneys with the broken side mirror and spun him around to get a shot at staking his heart. Poor kid didn't see me coming. I almost felt sorry for him. Almost.

A group of sheriff deputies (who all also happened to be werewolves) came out of the courthouse. No wonder the vampires smelled wolves nearby. Larry appeared to be leading the charge. The deputies were running to their service vehicles. I hopped in Larry's truck before he peeled out of the parking lot after the two vamps that got away.

Larry nodded to me when we got closer to the left-over motorcycle gang. I leaned up from where I was reaching for a stake I had left in Larry's truck. It must have gotten kicked under the front seat the last time I was in here. I nodded back telling him I was ready.

27

He and I had gone hunting so many times together we didn't need to talk to know what the other was going to say.

Larry pulled up next to the vampire leader. I threw my door open, hitting the vamp. He veered off course slightly. That was enough for me to be able to do my job. I jumped onto the back of his bike from my perch on the passenger seat of Larry's truck. He was trying to steer and elbow me off at the same time. It wasn't working out so well for him. It was going great for me though.

I made a hand signal to Larry who slacked off the accelerator letting one of his motorcycle deputies, Deputy Franklin from his build, get next to me. I climbed under the arm of the vampire motorcycle gang so I was sitting on his lap facing him. That would have been hot if he wasn't a psycho killer. Who am I kidding? This is me we're talking about. It was still hot.

I staked the vamp with the actual proper silver stake I had found in Larry's truck. Good thing I was such a hot mess I left my weapons all over the place. I had about three seconds after this vamp turned to dust to grab the arm of the werewolf deputy riding next to me so I didn't crash and burn with the dead vampire's motorcycle. As far as I knew, burning me alive (or dead) would keep me dead just like it did for witches, vampires and just about anything else. We had never tried it. I wasn't too keen to find out if my theory was right or not. At least I wasn't keen on it now. I flipped back and forth between wanting to end it all because I was just so tired all of the time and wanting to stay alive and fight the good fight. Fiery death just wasn't my style anyway. Plus, now I had a mysterious origin story to figure out.

I knew everyone on the road watching me was holding their breath as I grabbed Deputy Franklin's arm. I sure was. Deputy Franklin was a good guy and an even better deputy. It was easy for him to grab my arm and lift me off the vampire's motorcycle while still steering his own motorcycle. I had enough training to be able to right myself on the back of his bike without making us crash or falling off and getting run over by Larry. Had that happened, it would have been the second time he killed me today. I wasn't too keen to let him kill me again so soon.

I looked behind me. Four deputies were flanking the second vampire. It looked like they were just playing with their dinner. Deputy Franklin made a U-turn on the barren two lane highway out of town to take us back to town. When we were clear of the other deputies, the two deputies in front of the motorcycle peeled away from the chase so the two deputies behind the motorcycle could come up next to the vampire. Both deputies grabbed the vampire at the same time and sped away. The vampire was torn in half. They let his motorcycle crash into a tree on the side of the road.

Someone would clean that up later.

Deputy Franklin let me off at the front of the courthouse then gave a small wave as he drove away. He was probably on duty and needed to get back to work. Larry got out of his truck to frown at me in person.

"Selene, just because you can't die doesn't mean you should be so reckless." Larry sighed rubbing his sizable belly.

Every time he did that I had to stifle a laugh. Larry looked like a pregnant lady who was about to give birth any minute. You would think being a werewolf would do something for your physique. It does not. How you look when you're turned is how you look for the rest of your life- natural or otherwise. It didn't matter how much you worked out or ate right. You stayed the same. Granted, you got supernatural speed and strength out of the deal, but, still.

"Larry, you know me, I never look for trouble. It just always manages to find me." I threw my hands up in the air to show him I was just as exasperated by my antics as he was.

"It's called back-up and it's not there for you to only use when it suits you." Larry put his arm around my shoulder.

I could tell he was using some of his werewolf strength to squeeze me nice and tight. It was oddly comforting. Something dawned on me. I still didn't know how I died last night.

"Larry, you never did tell me how I died." I craned my neck, twisting in his supernatural grip.

29

He squeezed me once hard enough to re-break anything that had already healed on my body from my fight with the vamps. "Well, hon, that's because I don't know. A buddy of mine, Marcus, you remember him? He runs the cop shop and the pack up in the city despite his broken heart? Anyway, he called me about a young lady who died very publically for no discernable reason." Larry paused and looked down at me. "That'd be you, sweetie."

Obviously. I rolled my eyes. I knew he was talking about me. I was the only one who could die in a very public way then come back to life just so I could top myself the next time I died.

Larry steamrolled through my eye roll and kept explaining. "Anyway, Marcus said there was so much blood and your shirt was cut in several places, they thought you'd been stabbed. When the medics looked at you, there were no stab wounds. We cooked up a fake case to get your body shipped down here." Larry seemed right proud of himself.

"What kind of case? Am I wanted dead or alive?" I nudged him in the stomach with my elbow.

He rolled his eyes. "Matter of fact, little lady, we made you look like the suspect in a string of high end robberies round these parts." Larry leaned back a little. If he had been wearing suspenders he would have grinned and hooked his thumbs through them.

"The only thing high end around here are the cows. Did you make me a cattle rustler?" I was starting to get a little screechy. I didn't exactly have a good name but I took offense at it being sullied like this. In these parts cattle rustling was worse than murder (which I committed on a frequent basis).

Larry shrugged. "Maybe, we very well couldn't make you the victim of a serial killer. That would have brought the feds on us like hogs to slop."

It was my turn again to roll my eyes. I had been standing still too long. My hands were itching for a job especially now that I had a stake in them. Dusk was starting to settle on the fringes of the town. I would have to do less skulking on my way to the local bar, *The Tipsy*

Cow, than I would have in broad daylight. Reggie was on the only lead I had. He would find me when he found anything useful. I didn't have anything else to do but wait. I may have mentioned before- I hate waiting.

"Well, Lar, I've got some place to be." I clapped his back with a lot less force than he had exerted on mine earlier and turned to head down Main Street.

"At least let me drive you down to the Tipper." Larry spun me around to face his truck.

"Fine. If you come in to get a drink with me let me talk to the low-lives. I need a job. Mama's gotta get her mojo back." I climbed into his truck.

"You can't get back what you never had." Larry grinned as he buckled his seat belt and started the engine.

I opened my mouth to say something clever but decided to buckle my seatbelt instead. That was a good burn and I was going to let him have it. Plus, I didn't have any kind of comeback at the ready.

Chapter 4

I dodged the lights of the few cars leaving the bar creating traffic at three AM on a small town weekend night. I cut between the back of an apartment building and the back of the bar next door that I had just exited not of my free will. Garth, the owner/bartender/bouncer, had kicked me out after I did not (yes, my fingers are crossed right now) start a fight with a cheesy knock off necromancer over the soul of the guy slumped over the end of the bar. After leaving out the back, as I was sometimes accustomed to do, I decided to head home. If you could call Asylum home.

I wonder if, out in that dark grimy alley, my soul was being called back to my past. If I hadn't shown up when I did he probably would have died. Let me back up here. When I rounded the corner between being almost home and someplace I could never go again, I saw the guy bleeding out on a heap of full trash bags. He had beautiful chocolate skin and the most intense amber eyes I have ever seen.

For a split second he reminded me of someone I once knew. I couldn't place him. It didn't matter if I knew him or not. It actually didn't matter if his wounds were demon-related or caused by stupid humans. It was my job to protect this town. I had actually sworn an oath in an official ceremony in front of a ton of people. Larry first told me he was proud of me that day. It was kind of a big deal. I mean, I'm kind of a big deal, so, you know, it worked out.

It wasn't like I had time to place where I knew him from anyway. Two shadows blinked into existence behind the guy still lying

32

prone over garbage. His eyes were closed now. There was no point in shouting for him to watch out for the inky figures slinking in the shadows. The growling started when the two figures stopped pacing circles around their prey and turned their attention to me.

Hellhounds.

Damn.

I didn't have any weapons on me that would kill a hellhound. I'm also pretty sure I either left my silver stake in the ladies room or lost it playing cards with backwater dirtbags. I patted my jacket pockets. Yeah, not even a stake on me. Like it would have done me much good, but still.

The half- dead guy was wearing a ceremonial loincloth. The markings designing the edges looked Egyptian. I didn't care. I could see his bare chest rise and fall. He would have to wait. There were more pressing matters at hand.

I had to keep the attention of the hellhounds off this guy. I would be the one to judge him and his intentions, not the master of the beasts gnashing their teeth at me, a stark white contrast in the darkness I now found myself in.

Did the street lights go out when the hellhounds arrived or had they been off this whole time? I really needed to stay out of my head and start paying more attention to my surroundings. Maybe I should also drink less. Nah, that would be crazy.

Score. If I concentrated, I found I was able to see in the dimness somewhat. Enough to see the gold hilt of a ceremonial weapon with an onyx blade glittering between me and the hellhounds. I didn't care that I was about to desecrate a ritual artifact. I would answer for that and many other crimes in hell later. Not today.

I bent down and palmed an empty soda can. I waited until the hellhounds stopped pacing before I threw the can down the alley. One hellhound trotted off to see what all the commotion was about. The other guarded the unconscious man watching his partner's back in the distance. I sprinted to the knife slipping in alley grime.

33

Shit.

I was on my back still when I heard the scout hound running in my direction. I leaned up on my elbows and looked in my hand. I had the knife. Sprinting wasn't my forte, however, slipping to the exact spot I needed to grab the only weapon that might kill hellhounds was.

The hellhound was stupid enough to take a flying leap over the guy and his trash couch to get to me. I laid back and used its mistake to my advantage. I laterally sliced the underbelly of the hellhound from throat to guts. That was enough to send it back to whatever plane of existence it came from. I put my arm over my face to keep hellhound ash out of my eyes and mouth.

The second hellhound must have been head of its class at Hell University because he wasn't as easily dispatched as his dumbass friend. Or maybe I wasn't smarter than a hellhound. Either way, this hellhound ran through the falling ashes of his beast friend to attack me while I was getting up. A rush of air pushed me backward making me feel like my soul had left my body for a split second. At first, I thought the hellhound's massive black paw scattered my soul on the wind with the ashes of the other hellhound. In reality, all it did was hit me in the face with its paw and send me flying into the back wall of the bar.

Pieces of brickwork followed me down to the ground to lay next to the guy who started this whole shit show. We laid there covered in blood and alley slime. He was unconscious. I was getting there. This was a thousand percent not good. My remarkable healing abilities did not also make me fast. Whatever mutated gene or magic spell I got to be able to heal did not mutate enough to make me move at a rate faster than a sloth in a snowstorm especially compared to supernatural creatures like vampires and hellhounds.

I could use some speed right now. That was the only way I was going to be able to defeat this one. I heard a growl and felt sticky dog breath through the leg of my jeans. I didn't even want to open my eyes to be a party in my second death in as many days. Fuck it. If he kills me I'll come back. Or live in hell forever. The only thing stopping me from actually dying was the guy I was supposed to be saving. I heard a dog yelp as I struggled to sit up and defend our position against the onslaught of fur and teeth that had forced me down in the first place. I

34

immediately regretted every decision I had ever made in my life, most specifically the one to sit up just now.

The alley swam before my eyes. A rough hand helped me up. The guy had healing abilities to rival my own? I looked down at my feet. No. That Egyptian guy was still taking his death lying down. I could have really used his help right about now. It looked like the only thing he was going to be good for tonight was accidently dropping a dagger in a not terrible place.

"Stay here."

I couldn't focus on who had said that, on who had just propped me against a crumbling brick wall to wait while they finished the job I started. I closed my eyes and steadied my breathing. I probably shouldn't have done so many shots of mixed liquor earlier. When in Rome though, am I right? I opened my eyes again and found I could finally focus. The voice belonged to the shape of a six foot man in a black duster who moved a whole lot faster than me even when I wasn't concussed.

He killed the last hellhound with the onyx dagger before turning to me. He had a hood pulled over his face. I couldn't see all of his features clearly. I could tell he had a few battle scars from old wounds on his hands.

He walked toward me, stepping over the guy who had slept through the whole fight scene. Big and Tall thought better of it and turned his back to me while he stooped to check the man's pulse. Satisfied, he took three more steps toward me and pulled his hood down first, waiting for my reaction. His face was scarred with just as many old wounds as his hands. It didn't detract from the rugged good looks hiding underneath all the scars. He didn't stop there. He took off his coat revealing his arms under his black t-shirt.

I gasped this time. I couldn't help it. He had more than just a few battle scars. His whole body looked like he had been pieced together like a jigsaw puzzle of the human variety. If his scars weren't startling enough, his eyes sealed the deal. The blue of his irises was indescribable. Ocean. Sapphire. Cerulean. None of that could ever describe the beauty held in the deep pools of his eyes. I wanted to get lost in his eyes for the rest of my life then die there. Heaven would be continuing to live there with him in the world behind his eyes. I needed to focus on what just happened with the hellhounds instead of getting lost in a place I had no business getting lost in the first place.

I must have swayed a little. He stepped closer to steady me with his muscular arms. I let his sapphire eyes bore into mine for a split second before I acted like the bat shit crazy lady that I am.

"I totally had this." I punched the conscious guy in the arm. I could have sworn I heard my hand shattering into a thousand pieces. That's what I get for trying to be funny- a broken hand.

He just stood there and took it.

The sudden movement of letting my true nature come out did not help either the hangover I could feel coming on or the concussion from hell that just would not go away. I decided not to move any more. The alley had stopped spinning like a ride at the state fair but I couldn't peel myself away from wall-flowering the back wall of the bar.

"My name is..."

He was so close I could smell his sweat. He didn't wear cologne, just his natural musk. I could feel his body heat warming my soul, taking me to a place I hadn't been in so long.

"Cassius," I breathed.

~

"Selene, Octavian's armies are coming for me. I won't let them take us for his own perverse pleasure. I have a plan. I will need your help." My mother was back in my memories looking much the same as she did in the last memory I had of her. The only difference was this time she wore a turquoise dress.

I heard my voice answer her, "My lady, what can I do?"

The queen of this age laid out a plan to get asps into her monument where we were currently making our last stand against Octavian and his armies. She didn't seem to be worried about dying. She was more worried about what her usurper would do to her before he granted her the serenity that only death might bring.

"You will be the key. Octavian's guard, Cassius, is in love with you. Only you can get him to let the asps in. He is the only one loyal to Octavian who will let us die with dignity." She whispered her plan to me as she searched the room for something. She found a small piece of parchment and pressed it into my hand. The concern in her eyes moved me. She was telling me a plan that would get us killed. I had to be fine with this place because worse things were about to happen. This was her way of saving us, of saving me. It was the only way. She had forgiven me for not marrying Alexander and ascending to her throne. I felt so sure of it.

"Yes, my lady." My feet walked toward the door of our self-made prison. It was constantly guarded by at least two of Octavian's Roman soldiers.

My mind was having trouble figuring out why I would want to die with my queen when the man I loved would still live. I got to the door. The first guard looked at me like I was a dead lizard on the bottom of his sandal. The second had piercing blue eyes and a kind smile. He looked incredulous I would stand here not because he hated me and what I stood for but because he loved me and was trying to protect me. We both knew it was a losing battle. That's why I had to die with my queen instead of living with my soul mate. The only way I could find peace in the Afterlife was to let this life go.

"What are you doing, scab?" Cassius grabbed me by the waist with one hand pushing me against the far wall out of earshot of the other guard. He pretended to choke me with his other hand.

I kept up pretenses by sobbing at his touch. Whispering, I said, "Get this note to Charmion. When she comes back with a last meal, you be the one to inspect the basket. Be careful of the contents for they will bring an end to this war."

I could see his eyes. He knew what we meant to do and that he shouldn't stop it. I could tell this decision would kill us both in different ways. "I'll be back for you later," he shouted, pulling the note out of my tunic as he pushed me to the ground. "Get back in your prison with your filthy queen."

I crawled away. I knew Cassius would give Charmion the letter to our freedom. I felt confident telling my queen that her will would be done. I spent the day doing mindless chores waiting for my love to come back to me. At nightfall, Cassius did come back, pretending to be drunk. The two soldiers who had replaced Cassius and his compadre around mid-afternoon let Cassius in. They didn't care what he would do to us as long as he didn't kill us. Octavian wanted us alive so he could torture us and break our bodies and minds in front of our people. Cassius stumbled into the monument singing a war time ode loudly.

"My lady Cleopatra," his voice dripped with sarcasm and loathing. My queen knew this game. We had been playing it for the last several days. Cassius grabbed my arm making a show of being rough with me.

"Let me be." I pretended to try and get out of his grip.

"Let her go. Whatever you would do to her, do unto me instead." Cleopatra knew of our love. One of her last acts as my queen and mother was to break convention and let me be with the man I loved even if it was only for one night.

"Don't worry, Your Highness. You're next." Cassius yelled for the other guards' benefit. To Cleopatra he whispered, "The basket will come at noon tomorrow. Be prepared."

Cleopatra gave a slight nod of acknowledgment. The other guards gave up watching the show and went back to their posts giving us the privacy we needed.

"Stand before me," Cleopatra commanded.

We did as we were told.

"Face each other and join hands." Cleopatra took a small parchment from inside her robes.

She was performing a hurried version of a traditional wedding ceremony. She had not told me she was planning that. I was giddy with excitement. I would not spend my afterlife in torment now as an unwed virgin destined to wander Purgatory until I found my true love.

38

"Do you, Cassius, take Selene for eternity?"

"I do." He smiled at me. For the first time in a long time I knew everything would be alright and that we would see each other again.

"Do you, Selene, take Cassius for eternity?"

"I do." I smiled back at him.

"I now pronounce you husband and wife. Now, go. I have prepared a honeymoon suite for you." Cleopatra shooed us out of the main hall to a small room she had adorned with furs and silks.

Cassius and I hurried into our room before the other guards investigated the quiet. We spent our last night together as husband and wife. Day broke too soon. We watched the sun rise, resigned to our fates. After we had gotten dressed, I pulled Cassius closer desperate for the warmth of his skin on mine one last time.

Cassius took my hands out of his tunic kissing them. "I have to report for my shift. I'm sorry. We will spend eternity together. I will find a way. I promise." He turned to leave.

"Wait!" I hurried across the room to him.

"Selene, I can't stay." Cassius put his hands up to stop me.

"I know. It's just," my hands flailed in the air while I tried to find the right words, "my mom is up to something. I think this bracelet is the key to the whole thing." I pulled a gold bracelet with emeralds, diamonds, rubies and opals piled high in an elaborate scarab design out of my tunic pocket. "Hide it somewhere we will find it when we come back to this world, together I hope." I pressed the bracelet I had stolen from my mother earlier into Cassius's hands.

He nodded and hid the bracelet in his tunic. His rapid stride out of our marriage suite didn't hide the fact that he was wiping tears from his face before going outside to report for duty. I didn't shame him for his emotion. I was wiping tears from my face as well.

Cleopatra and I waited. At noon, Cassius brought in a basket slamming it hard on the table. "Lunch." His eyes lingered on mine one last time before he turned away hunching his shoulders, feeling just as defeated by circumstance as I did.

"It's time." Cleopatra put her hand on my shoulder to strengthen my resolve.

We stood together as I opened the basket releasing the asps. One immediately sprang to strike clenching its teeth on Cleopatra's breast like a baby seeking its last meal. I held my arm out straight closing my eyes waiting for the second one to strike. The last thing I felt before my eyes stayed closed for good was the stinging bite of the snake and the fire of the poison coursing through my veins until it reached my heart in two beats.

~

I woke up on the rotting hardwood floor of an abandoned apartment. I suspected it was the apartment building behind the bar I had been evicted from last night mostly because scents of urine and vomit weighed heavily on every part of the room suffocating me like I was in a greenhouse filled with poison. I tried not to gag and add to what was already in the air. I pushed a heavy coat off of me and got up. The passed out Egyptian guy was with me and he was awake now. And way more excited to see me than I was to see him. I was more interested in the other guy who may or may not still be my husband. I had to get through the half-naked Egyptian guy first.

"My lady," the guy bowed low touching the ground with his forehead.

"Yeah, I'm a lady alright. What's your deal, guy? Why were the hellhounds after you last night?" I was tired, hungry and craving the touch of a man I just met last night that I had apparently met ages ago. I mean, how old was Cleopatra? At least a thousand years? Two thousand? Let's put aside the fact that she's also my mother making me at least that old too. Not a gray hair in sight though. At least I had that going for me.

"Anubis, my lady. I am forever in your debt for sparing my life last night. Osiris sent hellhounds to bring me back to the Underworld. I could not go back knowing my goddess of the moon was in danger." Anubis grabbed my hand holding on tighter than I could break free from. "My lady, your brother, Alexander, is coming for you. He wants to serve justice upon you for what you did to the lady, Baht."

It took some doing before I was able to wrench my hand free from his. All the while my husband just stood there watching. I could have sworn he was smirking as he enjoyed the show. We were only married for one night, according to the memory seeing him last night unlocked. I wondered if we would have had a good marriage had we been married and together all this time. I also wondered how he got all of those scars. He hadn't had them in my memory of him.

"I don't know what you are talking about. I'm no goddess. I don't even know who you are." I turned my back on my loyal servant to yell at my husband. "And you, who do you think you are? Where have you been? Are we still married?"

"You remember me and not Anubis? Curious. What all do you remember?" Cassius grabbed my shoulders shaking me gently. When his body touched mine goosebumps pushed their way to the surface of my skin causing me to shiver. We moved closer to each other sharing heat and the memory of our bodies touching in places our clothing now covered. Cassius leaned down and kissed me. Passion washed over us taking me back to another time.

~

I'm standing on the dark cobblestone street hiding behind something. A barrel? I'm hiding behind a barrel? Really? What time period am I in? I looked down. I was wearing a corset and hoop skirt with an overcoat that covered every inch of me. Just for overkill's sake I was also wearing boots that went up to my ankles and gloves that went all the way up my arms. I'm surprised I wasn't also wearing some sort of fascinator with a veil so none of my skin showed in public or got any sun. Okay, who am I kidding? My skin rarely got sun nowadays. Why would the past be any different?

Things were happening so fast I had a hard time telling what was going on. A pack of hellhounds sauntered out of view shimmering between this dimension and the one they lived. A man in a stark white coat stained with blood stepped into focus. The man hunched over something. I moved closer, creeping up behind him, not wanting to spook him even though I knew this was a memory and he couldn't see me. When I got closer I saw beyond where the man was standing.

Cassius was lying on the ground being tended to by the man in the white coat. He must have been a doctor of some kind. The mangled bloody heap writhed in pain on the ground. I wouldn't have known it was Cassius but his short black hair and blue eyes were the only features that weren't damaged in some way. This must have been how he got all of his scars. Judging by the dress of the other people standing around us staring in open-mouthed horror, this had happened at least two hundred years ago. My hand instinctively went to my belly which I realized was swollen with pregnancy.

Cassius was trying to say something. I rested my hand on the doctor's shoulder so I could lean in to hear Cassius's dying words.

"Selene." Cassius choked out along with some blood that shouldn't have been in his mouth in the first place. "Victor, protect Selene."

He looked past the man standing above him. He stared into my eyes like he could see me there even though that, like most other things in my life, should have been impossible. Then, he died. When Cassius closed his eyes I realized I had been clutching something to my chest. It was a parcel wrapped in brown paper. Seemed about right for the time period I found myself in.

"Victor, take the book. Use it to save him." I handed the parcel to Victor and ran.

I ran until I was out of breath, choking on what little air was coming into my body. My stomach spasmed. I was having contractions.

"Hello, Selene." I turned toward the voice behind me. The voice belonged to a man I recognized now, a man I realized I hadn't seen in a very long time. My brother. Alexander.

~

"Selene," Cassius stood in front of me in present day trying to get my attention. It took me a second to come to my senses and see that I was back in the apartment choking on stale air not trying to catch my breath from the unexpected run I had just taken. In my memory, I thought Cassius had died. By all rights he should have died that night. His wounds were severe enough that he should not have lived long enough to talk to Victor, whoever he was. Here was Cassius though, concerned about me when it was me who should have been concerned about him.

"How did you survive? Why haven't we been together all this time? How old am I? What is happening to me?" I threw my hands up in frustration. After the second memory, I had realized I didn't actually know anything about myself. My entire life had been a lie. A lie that I couldn't even remember most of. I walked out the front door of the apartment willing myself to want answers less and less with each step toward my future I took.

"Same old Selene." Cassius carried me over the threshold of my old life like he had carried me into our bridal suite on our wedding night.

Anubis had folded the duster into a sort of cushion for me to sit. Cassius gently set me down sitting next to me on my right side. We leaned against the bare living room wall.

I waited for him to say something. He didn't. Anubis did, making me think that maybe, moon goddess or not, I needed a man-servant in my life.

"My lady-" Anubis was on his knees at my feet. His gaze never quite met my eyes.

I put my hand up to stop him. If this was how it was going to be I wasn't having any part of it. "Selene. My name is Selene. Stop

43

with the 'my lady' business. We aren't wherever you are from. I don't have the time or patience to follow antiquated rules." I sat up straighter and tried to look commanding. I guess it worked.

"Of course, Sel-Selene." Anubis looked at me like I was about to deck him.

Cassius shook his head and laughed.

"We need to go before your brother finds us. The sunlight is his domain. After all, while he is your twin he is still your opposite. You are goddess of the moon and thus any creature ruled by night as such is under your control. As the god of the sun, Alexander controls those ruled by its light." Anubis looked out the window while he talked to me.

Anything not to look me in the eyes I guess. Or, maybe he was checking for Alexander. Anubis was right. I did better at night, felt more energized, even fought better. Normally, if I wasn't sleeping all day I wasn't doing much unless I had to.

"What does that even mean? 'Those ruled by the moon'?" I spun Anubis away from the window to look at me.

"Those ruled by the moon are supernatural. Think your shifters, vampires, ghouls and the like. Basically, those ruled by the sun are humans. You protect the shadows, Alexander holds dominion over the daylight." Cassius turned to look behind him through the bare window like he thought Alexander had a sniper riffle trained on us at this very second.

Geez these guys needed to cool it with this window. They were giving me heart palpitations.

"While I don't quite remember the details of anything from my past, I do remember about two hundred years ago I had a baby and Cassius died." I turned from the window everyone was so keen to look out of and grabbed Cassius's arm.

I had a baby. Where was it? Was it a boy or a girl? Was it alive? Wouldn't you think that I would remember something about giving birth? Shouldn't I be able to remember *anything* about my life?

"We should take you home." Cassius grabbed my arm dragging me away from the window.

"I'm not going back to Vampireville until I get some answers." I pushed him against the wall. The drywall cracked. It didn't rain pieces of chalk dust around him like the brickwork had crumbled around me last night. "Cassius, what aren't you telling me?"

"Selene," Cassius looked at Anubis.

Anubis stared at the floor. "Actually, he goes by Adam now. He has ever since the night Alexander set a pack of hellhounds on him and kidnapped you." Anubis looked up. Tears were pooling in the corners of his eyes.

"Your baby died a long time ago." Cass- I mean Adam, he goes by Adam now, waited for me to react.

I couldn't. I didn't know what to say. I didn't know what to do. For the first time in my life (that I could remember) I did nothing. I felt nothing. I was nothing.

"Selene," Adam grabbed my arm.

Despite not wanting to feel anything, when Adam touched me my entire body shivered in anticipation.

"We need to go." Adam held me to his chest.

I had never found comfort in another person before. Until now.

Anubis was starting to panic. "My lady, I mean Miss Selene, it is my sworn oath to protect you. When I escaped my prison cell, I left to find you despite my allegiance to Lord Osiris."

"Why is it your sworn duty to protect me?" I hoped my face looked as skeptical as I felt.

"You are the goddess of the moon. As a werewolf, my allegiance lies with you and you alone. You have been missing for two millennia. I am not the only one who will benefit from your return."

"So all werewolves have to do what I say?" A thought was forming in my brain that I couldn't stop.

"Yes, my lady. We are sworn from birth to protect you with our lives." Anubis was back to kneeling on the ground at my feet.

Now I knew why the Sheriff felt the need to parent me all the time. The Sheriff. I had to make a phone call. "Either of you boys got a cell phone?"

Adam reached over Anubis to grab something out of his coat pocket. We needed to get back to Asylum without being seen. I knew just the werewolf for the job. I dialed a number I knew by heart. Sheriff Larry picked up on the third ring.

Chapter 5

Sheriff Larry drove us to the back of the courthouse in the town's main square. Adam got out first and helped me out of the Sheriff's SUV. Anubis trailed me like he was my puppy, which, if you think about it, he kind of was if he was a werewolf and I was a moon goddess. The Sheriff brought up the rear. Apparently James had every able-bodied supernatural in town looking for me last night. No one thought to look in the only place I was likely to be- the bar. This was going to be a real shit show, but I had to face James some time even if it was just long enough to grab a fake passport and hitch a ride to the airport.

I picked a stone to our left that looked one imperceptible shade darker than the rest and pressed it. How I picked it out from the rest of the stones on the first try I'll never know. Normally I pressed all the stones in the general area of the one I needed and kept pressing until I got it right.

A tunnel opened to our right revealing a staircase leading down to nowhere. I peered down the tunnel before going in. I always expect it to turn into a portal to hell and swallow me whole every time I have to come here. It was actually just a random stone tunnel with the same lit torches in sconces like the tunnel I had used earlier to make my escape from Reggie's personal library.

I led the boys through the length of the tunnel until we reached the end. It didn't take very long. We were just under the foundation of the courthouse. The cavern the tunnel opened up into the same library

Reggie had spirited me out of the day before. We were just coming in from a different direction than the one I had taken to leave.

James was standing in the middle of the room with his hands in his pants pockets looking annoyed. Good, I was in my normal amount of trouble then, which was not as much as I thought I would be.

"Where have you been? And who are these clowns?" James turned to walk to his office. He expected us to follow. We did not disappoint.

"Anubis is my werewolf servant and Adam is my husband." I mimed a nasty face at James while his back was turned.

He surprised me by swiftly turning around and both seeing the childish face I was making and making me run into his solid chest. He sighed, opened his mouth to admonish me, decided better of it then kept walking. James didn't yell at workers or servants in front of other workers and servants. He was actually a pretty good boss when he wasn't being a dick by purposefully sending me on missions where I had to wade through the sewers or face a slime monster without backup. Then again, all the vampires I'd ever met were uppity dicks so maybe he wasn't so great just because he had a little decorum and diplomacy.

We were following James down a long hall. It was different from the tunnel we used to come into Asylum. It still had sconces every few feet or so. These walls were made of wood paneling instead of stonework. In between the sconces were large portraits of people in fancy dress clothes wearing crowns. James stopped at the last door on the right. By the door was a picture of James wearing a crown and a cape. He was holding a large horn in one hand and a scepter in the other. He ran Asylum which meant he was the sort of king or president or whatever. I thought he was more of a dick, I mean dictator. I didn't care for office politics much, especially politics that involved ancient beings like vampires. Also, who puts a picture of themselves in a hallway for all to see if they weren't full of themselves?

James led us into a private chamber I had never been in before. It looked like his bedroom. I didn't know where to stand. I had never willingly entered a man's bedroom. Thankfully it was well-kept so dirty underwear didn't assault my eyes and the general malaise of man smells didn't send me running in the opposite direction.

There was a four-poster bed with a thick red velvet canopy and curtains you could draw around the entire bed. For privacy, I guess. There was a chaise lounge at the foot of the bed and huge wood furniture covering every wall. I couldn't tell you what kind of furniture it was. They all looked like chifforobes to me. I had no clue why a guy would need so many free standing closets. It kind of reminded me of all of the television shows about royal families getting busy in the bedroom. This was always what their bedrooms looked like.

Adam and I sat in the two padded wooden desk chairs in front of James. Anubis stood directly behind me like he was trying to protect me from an assault from behind. Sheriff Larry leaned against a far wall actually keeping quiet for once. He didn't really need to be here but he loved spectator sports and this was sure to be the best show he would ever see.

James sat for so long before speaking Anubis started to shift from foot to foot, uncomfortable from standing in the same potion for too long. "Where have you been?"

"Getting mauled by hellhounds and finding out I'm an ancient Egyptian goddess. No, wait, *confirming* that I am an ancient Egyptian goddess *and* the daughter of Cleopatra who is back and wants to take over the world or something." I crossed my arms over my chest. This was going to be one hell of a long interrogation for him. He was hiding something. I could tell by the way he shifted his eyes away from me. "My turn." I took a stab in the dark and guess what he might be guilty of. "How long have you known who I was? How long have you been withholding the truth from me?"

"That was two questions." James leaned back in his padded leather desk chair looking like the cat who ate the canary and was subsequently praised for doing so. "I suspected you were part of the goddess of the moon's bloodline. I had no idea you were the *actual* goddess of the moon. Remember shortly after the third time you died and came back when you finally started working for me and stopped working against me? You excelled at calming down newly turned wolves and bringing them in unlike any other before you except for the goddess of the moon herself. I had no proof until now. Anubis is bound to the goddess of the moon. His presence alone is proof enough for me."

I stared into James's eyes for as long as I could stand it. The jade of his irises seemed to turn black for a second like Mitch's had when the demon in him decided to come out and play. "You're lying to me about something and I'm going to find out what it is."

James gave Anubis a small shrug and a look that seemed to say "we're in this together, pal. Don't rat me out."

I whipped around in my chair to stare Anubis down. "You told me earlier you just broke out of prison. Is that why I haven't met you before today?"

"You have met me before today. I have been your loyal servant since you were born. When you and your mother, Pharaoh Cleopatra, died I dressed your bodies for burial. Alexander told me he was going to use *the Book of the Dead* to bring you back. I should not have trusted a sun god so readily." Anubis hung his head in shame.

I could actually smell the synapses in my brain burning from trying to figure out the confusing and sordid details of my life. I patted his hand. "Thank you for protecting me and breaking all of the rules to get me back. I'm sorry you were imprisoned because of me."

"The legend surrounding Selene, goddess of the moon, is incomplete. From what I gathered, goddess Selene died with her mother, Cleopatra. After, her body was subsequently used to house the soul of her brother's dead wife, Baht. There were rumors that Selene wasn't dead during this process. If that is true then the reason why you have lived so long without retaining memories of your lifetimes is because you have two souls in your body." James shuffled the papers on his desk either trying to look authoritative or just needing something to do with his hands.

"Hot damn!"

We all turned to look at Sheriff Larry. I had forgotten he was in the room until his little outburst. Judging by everyone else's reactions,

I think they forgot about him too. To his credit, Larry looked embarrassed as hell. I smiled. Larry was always good for a laugh or a quick pick me up.

I stood up and began pacing the small space in front of James's desk. "Based on Reggie's research and the memories I started having yesterday, I am going to go out on a limb and say I am Selene, goddess of the moon, and that something weird is definitely going on. Whether it's because I have two souls in my body or not, I'm the last person who could tell you." I stood behind Adam placing my hands on his massive shoulders, immediately warmed by the feel of him under my hands. I just wanted to be near him in every way possible.

"Where is Reggie anyway? The old coot owes me a poker game." Larry was still leaning against the wall. He had found a toothpick somewhere on his person and was using it to clean something out of his teeth. The moon wasn't full yet so he couldn't have gone hunting last night.

My stomach growled in envy. It had been a long time since I had eaten anything, longer if I had only stuck to a liquid diet at the bar last night.

James pursed his lips and looked at Anubis who looked down at the floor. "Reggie asked for some time off to visit his family. He should be back in a day or so."

I exploded all over the room in my traditional fashion. My pacing quickened and my hands flailed wildly in front of my body creating a small breeze that startled the papers on the desk. "What? He has had family this whole time and none of them have ever come to visit him? Why now? Why when I need him does he decide to do this? Why did you grant him the leave?"

James stood up straightening his tie. "Goddess of the moon or not, the world does not turn solely for you, Selene. Reginald does not have any biological family living. There is a small sect of griffins in hiding that he went to visit. Despite what you think and wrongly accuse me of constantly, I am not a monster." James finished admonishing me before he sat down again.

That was fine, Larry was there to pick up any slack in the conversation. "What about you, lover boy? Where do you fit in all this?" Larry was no longer holding up the wall since he came to stand between me and Adam.

Adam was nonplussed. He turned in his seat to stare up at Larry who was only taller than Adam because Adam was sitting. "After the hellhound attack, I woke up in Victor Frankenstein's lab. He was dead and Selene was gone. I mourned for longer than I should have before I began to look for her. I didn't realize she had given birth until it was much too late." Adam had a sorrow in his eyes that would always be there.

No amount of time would ever heal that wound.

I knew this from experience. I would always mourn the loss of my child, whether I remembered them eventually or not.

"I have been having memories since that demon attacked me in the morgue and I saw his tattoo."

"What tattoo? That wasn't in your report, Sheriff." James shuffled some paperwork on his desk to find the report he was referencing.

"I don't know what you mean, myself." Larry scratched the back of his head.

He probably didn't know about the tattoo. I had seen it then died. I hadn't had time to tell him about it. I still hadn't done my report or debrief of my time in the morgue. I was kind of hoping James had forgotten all about it. Paperwork was tedious and another one of those things that I hated. The way James looked at me now suggested he knew I still owed him a report. Or five.

James stared me down until I grew uncomfortable and told him what he wanted to know. "The demon in the morgue had a tattoo of a closed Eye of Horus. I started remembering random things after I saw it."

Adam pulled my arms tighter around his neck and started rubbing them.

James took an intake of breath so sharp I thought the air was going to cut his lungs on the way down. "That's why Reginald went to the griffins. The last time Cleopatra tried to start a revolution, a sect of griffins took her to Osiris in the Underworld and had her imprisoned. If there are new demons with her mark, she has risen from below and will try again."

"Where was Selene during the first revolution?" Larry was more interested in my past than I was.

"No one knew. Alexander and Baht in Selene's body were never found." James shrugged off Larry's question.

I guess there were just some things I was going to have to remember for myself. I was thrilled by that prospect because I'm not lazy and want everyone else to do everything for me at all.

Adam stood up and put his arms around me. "What's the last thing you remember?" Adam gently pushed some hair out of my face tipping my chin up so my eyes could meet his.

Every time I looked into his eyes I felt like I could see my past and my future. I felt like I could get so lost in there that I would never have to leave. His eyes were a place I wanted to stay. I wanted his arms to wrap around me so tightly I couldn't breathe. I wanted to be trapped in his embrace for eternity. I knew that might not be a possibility. We hadn't been together for at least two hundred years. I couldn't even remember him. What if we had a terrible relationship or left on bad terms? None of that mattered to me and that scared me. I shouldn't want someone this bad. I shouldn't have feelings for a man I had, essentially, just met. At this point in my life, I felt like my only option was to remain with the man I knew I loved even though I couldn't remember him. I knew there would never be anyone else for me.

"That was all I remembered. Our wedding night, my death alongside my mother and your death. I don't know who Baht is. I don't even know who I am. Not anymore." My eyes welled up without my permission.

I didn't know if it was the stress of the past few days or the fact that I just found out I was a mother without a baby. I hadn't felt right since I woke up in the morgue. I felt like something was off with my hormones and my brain wasn't firing quite right. There was something about my last death that was different. It felt like it should have been permanent. Something was holding me back from going to the Underworld for good.

Adam held me to his chest. I refused to be the girl who got emotional and cried every time something bad happened. I took a step back from him knowing if I laid on his chest I would never get back up. I needed him. I needed his love. I just didn't need his pity. I couldn't handle his pity.

"What's your plan, Selene?" James moved to sit on the front edge of his desk.

"I don't know. Kill a bunch of stuff, sleep, eat? Every day is the same. Every day I do things I don't remember doing. Every day I'm one step closer to death. Every day I'm one step closer to happiness." I shrugged and walked out of the room. I didn't want to continue this discussion. It seemed to be headed nowhere anyway. I had gotten everything I was going to from James. I would have to wait for Reggie to come back if I wanted more answers.

Adam caught my arm in the hallway where I was sprinting to my room with the unexpected urge to be free of this place once and for all. "You're just going to go about business as usual and ignore the rest of your life?"

"No. I'm going to go take a nap. Then, I'm going to kill a crap ton of bad stuff and ignore my life. Ignoring my problems always seemed to work the best for me in the past. This time should be no different." I patted Adam's arm.

We were at my suite now.

Adam ran his scarred hands through his jet black hair.

"Uh, so are you moving in here with me or are we not married anymore or what?" I felt like a moron asking my husband of two

54

thousand years if he was going to sleep with me tonight. I hadn't seen him in so long I didn't know him anymore.

"Do you think I should? I mean, if you want me to then I want to. I haven't held you near me in two hundred years. I missed you." Adam twirled the ends of my hair between his fingertips. His other hand grazed my cheek. My whole body felt like electric eels were using me as a charging station.

I didn't think it would be a bad idea to spend the night tracing the scars all over his body with my tongue but we had a lot to do. I felt like since I found out I was an immortal goddess, time was fleeting. I should have felt the opposite, like I had all the time in the world. With Cleopatra on the loose, I knew time was not something I had too much of.

"I can't just sit here in a windowless prison waiting for my mom or my brother to come kill me for what is probably a crazily dumb reason. I can't just sit here with a second soul in my body waiting to take over either. I don't know. I can't think right now. I don't want to think right now." Not like this. Not when you're touching me, I thought.

"Let me help you think." Adam had one arm around my waist and the other tangled in my hair. He leaned in to kiss me.

Instead of letting him, my body decided to pass out. I felt myself falling with no way to slow down the racing thoughts that flooded my mind.

~

I was looking up at the ceiling of a tomb. I only knew that because the symbols for Osiris, god of the Underworld, and the Eye of Horus, protector of royalty, were painted in white directly above me. I couldn't move my body. That should have worried me. I was too busy floating to be scared. I drifted in and out between this world and the next. The gates to the Afterlife wouldn't open for me. That meant Osiris didn't want me to join him. Odd for the god of the Underworld to not want a soul. Was something so wrong with mine that not even the keeper of souls wanted it?

I heard voices from behind me. Familiar voices of people who should not have been at my mummification. My mind sharpened. I was awake now and I still couldn't move. I was remembering my death. I guess since I didn't really die from snake poison I could have remembered this. How weird to remember your own funeral. Shouldn't someone have checked my pulse or something before trussing me up for entombment?

Alexander's footfalls strode into the room beseeched with some sort of spectacular purpose that could only be felt by my twin brother. The evil bastard. Alexander was followed by Anubis. I only knew that because Anubis was talking to Alexander. Anubis's footfall were that of a servant punished too often by his master- nonexistent.

Alexander stopped to stand in front of my body. He pushed a dark brown lock of hair out of his eyes with a hand that had seen more sun than my entire body. Alexander was forever messing with his hair. It was longer now than the last time I had seen him. He had not tried to visit mother and me in our prison. Alexander looked disheveled like he was actually distraught I was dead. Given the fact that Alexander hated me and I hated him, I don't think he cared that I had died. Evil oozed out of every pore in his body. He wasn't imbued with divine purpose like he thought. He was only imbued with nefarious purpose.

Anubis was next to him holding a book with a gold cover. It made sense for Anubis to be there. He had been my loyal servant since I was born. He served both me and Osiris now by ferrying my soul to the Underworld during the mummification process.

What was Alexander doing here though? It wasn't customary for family members of royalty to be present at mummification. In fact, where were all of the high priests who were supposed to be blessing my body? Had they all been capture by Octavius? Or worse, killed?

"Master Alexander, I got the Book of the Dead from Lord Osiris. I had to steal it. I know it will be worth it to bring back her majesty, Selene." Anubis bowed low to Alexander causing him to leave my limited line of sight.

"Open the book" Alexander commanded from behind my head. I couldn't see him anymore.

Anubis used a gold key with a scarab handle to open the book. The key looked like the one Reggie had used to open the secret door in the tunnel.

Alexander read out loud from one of the pages. My body began to spasm on the burial slab. The more spells Alexander used, the more animated my body became.

A black cloud swirled over me. A hand made out of obsidian fog reached out toward me. The hand coming out of the cloud turned into an arm attached to half a person. When the woman finally broke free of her prison I could see she wasn't the only soul in the swirling black mass. She was just the only soul to escape. When she escaped she went into my mouth.

My body stopped convulsing. After a split second I sat upright and smiled. It wasn't me smiling though.

"Baht, my beloved." Alexander came over to me helping my body off the burial slab.

"Alexander, my love." My body kissed Alexander passionately.

Now, I definitely knew it wasn't me in there. I never would have kissed Alexander like that. Baht was Alexander's dead wife. I wanted to shudder at the thought of what she and Alexander would do with my body to make up for lost time, only I couldn't because I was no longer in control of my own body.

"Master Alexander, you said you were bringing back Princess Selene. You lied to me. You will pay for your betrayal." Anubis dropped the Book of the Dead and took his ceremonial dagger out of his waistband.

He charged Alexander, dagger raised high ready to strike. Alexander side stepped causing Anubis to fall cutting my right arm in the process.

"Watch it, Alexander. I didn't get Selene's body to destroy it on the first day." Baht, in my body, was pissed. She ripped the hem of my burial dress to wrap my arm. I still have that scar on my right forearm. At least now I know how I got it.

Things were getting hazy. I was having a hard time focusing. Baht said in my voice, "Alexander, you moron, Selene is still in here. You should have waited for her soul to depart this world before you brought me back. She's fighting me. Do something."

Alexander picked up the book Anubis had dropped. Alexander had to step over Anubis's unconscious body to come back to mine. "Let's see if this will keep her dormant until I can find a way to send her to the Underworld for good."

Alexander started saying another spell from the book. I didn't hear all of it before I felt myself fade into obscurity.

~

I sat up in bed like I was running to keep Baht's soul from inhabiting my body. Adam was in bed beside me. He put one hand on the small of my back and the other on my chest. I tried to control my breathing. My breaths came out too ragged. I couldn't stop the flood from spilling out of my eyes if I wanted to. I clung to Adam hoping he would rescue me from my memories of my past, from myself.

I was scared and upset and I didn't care who knew it even though I normally worked incredibly hard every day not to have actual emotions. Emotions only slowed you down. Emotions made you feel like what the bad guy did wasn't really all that bad and he could be rehabilitated. Emotions made it seem like forgiving Alexander and not killing him outright was really an option when it so wasn't.

I was having a hard time with the fact that my own brother tried to kill me. Or, I guess he already thought I was dead so it was more like tried to use my dead body to house the soul of his evil wife. And now, I could not stop thinking about all of the disgusting things they did to each other while Baht was in my body. I wanted to vomit thinking about how Alexander's hands had touched me intimately and my hands had touched him back just as tenderly.

I hadn't forgotten about my baby. Knowing who Alexander really was and what he had already done to me, I wondered for the first time since learning I had even been pregnant if the baby I carried was mine and Adam's or Alexander and Baht's. I felt like even if the

58

baby wasn't truly mine I would still love it like I would have if I meant to be pregnant with it in the first place. Oh, God. I didn't even know if it was a boy or a girl. Of all of the memories that failed me why did this have to be one of them?

The heartbreak of my life was too overwhelming. I couldn't hold back the thoughts and feelings I had locked away any longer. The dam I had built around myself, around my heart, to keep me safe and protected from the world had finally burst. And there was no one to pick up the pieces and put me back together again. No one but the man who had been searching for me and loving me for two millennia.

Adam had given me what space he could since he found me yesterday. He never forced conversation on me. He never treated me like I should instantly love him because he never stopped loving me. He knew more about me than I knew about myself and he never made me feel like this was my fault. I wanted to ask him to stay in bed holding me for the rest of eternity. Part of me was afraid if I did he would say no. The other part of me was afraid he would say yes.

"Let it out. I don't know how you kept it together this long." Adam knelt beside me holding my hand.

Adam always looks at you with those impossibly honest eyes that make it so you can't help but tell him everything. I unleashed all of my hurt on him until there was nothing left.

"It's killing me to see you like this. I don't know what hurts me more- watching your suffering or having you feel like you're all alone when I'm right in front of you." He pulled me closer.

He just sat with me and held me and let me cry. For the first time in my life I felt acceptance and love. I never wanted to leave the safety of his arms. I never wanted to be in a place in my life again where I couldn't feel the coolness of his touch, where I couldn't lose myself in him only to realize I was never really lost in the first place.

Eventually I stopped crying. Eventually I stopped caring. Eventually I started living. I didn't want to fall in love with Adam all over again. I knew out of everything I had to do, including killing my mother and brother and stopping a revolution, at least one of those things would get me killed. I didn't want Adam to get caught up in the middle of that. I didn't want the things that happened in my past catch up with him instead of me.

The only way for us to be together was for me to recognize that without me in his life Adam had a checkered past too. Victor Frankenstein brought Adam back from death costing him his own life. When Adam woke up in 1818, people saw him as a monster not a confused man looking for his wife and child. He did a lot of things that earned him the title of monster, things he told me about now through his tears. We were both lamenting the mistakes of our pasts. We were both asking for forgiveness for our sins. We were both beyond absolution.

Now, it was those same scarred hands that had killed so many times before that were tenderly touching my face making me feel like we were the only two people in the world. I realized that even though I didn't remember a lot about him, I loved him and never wanted him to leave me again. I leaned in and kissed him. I think he was just as shocked as I was at my decision. His hand tangled itself in my hair like it had yesterday before my memories knocked me out of this time to another.

The longer the kiss went on, the more he touched me, my hair, my skin. It felt like fire coursing through my entire body. He was the electricity in my veins. He was the reason I was still here and not dormant in the shell of my former body.

Something in the back of my mind was trying to resist him. That piece of me wasn't strong enough to stop Adam from climbing into the bed with me. That nagging feeling turned into a diluted scream. It was Baht's soul trying to take control of my body again. I focused on Adam and our love until I drowned her out. I would deal with her later. She had taken so much from me I wasn't going to let her ruin my reunion with my husband.

I let Adam take me into his arms under the blankets and touch me like he had on our wedding night forgetting about all of my problems, forgetting about Baht and Alexander, forgetting that I was cursed with an evil second soul, forgetting about a baby that may or may not be mine.

Chapter 6

When I woke up I wasn't in bed with Adam. I was in the middle of the woods covered in blood. I sat up. The blood was just turning tacky. Whatever I had killed, I had done so recently. I had no memory of killing anything, of hunting demons or rogue wolves. I looked around me. The sun was just peeking through the trees. It hadn't been morning long. I hoped it was the morning after the last night I remembered. I felt older though like I had been gone for at least a few days. My mouth was dry. I was hungry. My body was stiff, my muscles too sore for just waking up after last night despite what Adam did to me.

I stood up and immediately fell back to my knees. Lying on the ground close to where I had woken up was a little girl with blonde ringlets. Her hair was stained with blood. One of the bows was missing from her pigtails. She wasn't moving.

I crawled to her praying she was still alive and I hadn't been the one to take her life. Her navy dress had turned dark with her blood. There were claw marks on her stomach and neck. Her mouth was opened in a silent scream. Her emerald eyes accused me of so much more than I knew I was even capable of.

I closed her eyes and my own. I laid my head on her lifeless body and sobbed. What had I done? Why didn't I know I had done it? Who was she? Were her parents missing her? She looked well cared for. I would miss her if she had been my child.

I stopped crying when the realization of what had happened finally dawned on me.

Baht.

I did not do this. My body may have been complacent in this crime when my mind was not my own. This was not me. Baht's soul took over my body and did this. What else had she done? Where was Adam? Oh, God, Adam. Did she kill him too? I had to get back to Asylum. I had to see for myself what kind of destruction Baht had wreaked on my life and the rest of the unsuspecting world. I had to find Alexander and kill him. I had to find *the Book of the Dead* and send Baht to the Underworld for good this time.

Where did I start? I spun in a circle. There was nothing around me except those kind of pine trees that stayed green all year. Wait. Was that water? Leaving the little girl behind was a hard decision for me. I knew I couldn't carry her and me out of here. She would have to wait. Like the rest of the world. If only the world would stop spinning until I got my shit together. That would be great. I was sprinting now. God, I hate running.

I found a shallow creek and washed up as best as I could. I knew if I followed the creek I would eventually find a road or a house. Which way should I go? Left or right? I'm right handed so I went right. It wasn't very scientific decision making process. It was the only way I was going to make a decision in that moment.

I didn't get far before stopping cold. Echoing through the trees was a cacophony of hysterical laughter. I couldn't tell where it was coming from. I started running again. I'm pretty sure we already covered how much I hate running.

I was out of breath trying not to slow down when the little girl with the blonde pigtails stepped in front of me. She was still laughing like a hyena on fire. I stopped in front of her panting hard. Did I check her pulse when I found her or did I assume she was dead because of all of the blood on her? Like most things in my life, I struggled to remember what happened ten minutes ago.

"Trying to figure out how I'm not dead right now? It's simple, dummy, I was never really alive in the first place." The little girl skipped ahead a few paces before turning back to see if I was following her.

I guess I didn't have a choice except to follow her. "What do you mean you were never alive at all?" I was still struggling to find my breath and keep up with the pace the little girl was skipping out in time.

"I came from the Underworld. Daddy found me there and called my soul to this place. It's much nicer here than it was there. Daddy gives me whatever I want." The little girl stopped skipping ahead and waited for me to catch up. When I did, she took my hand in hers leading us to wherever we were going. To Daddy, I assumed.

I assumed correctly. Turns out I should have gone left and followed the creek. I would have hit the road. Going right meant I would fall into Alexander's trap. He had a one room log cabin nestled in the woods. It looked quaint. I could have lived there with its dark green shutters and front porch swing if I didn't already know it belonged to my evil twin.

Alexander met us in the front yard. It killed me inside seeing Alexander, knowing what he had done.

"Don't think that way, Selene. Our life together wasn't entirely a lie. There were times in the past two millennia that we were friends." Alexander smiled warmly.

I took a step back from Alexander and the little girl and vomited all over Alexander's version of a happy home.

"Ophelia, what have you been feeding mommy?" Alexander picked me up and carried me into the bathroom of the cabin. Bathwater was drawn in the claw foot tub. It was still warm.

"She's not mommy anymore. She's Aunt Selene and Aunt Selene is no fun." Ophelia pouted.

Alexander was taking off my clothes. I tried to fight him. He laughed. We both knew I wasn't going to win any battles with him right now. Whatever Baht had done in my body had made it weak.

"Who is Ophelia? Who does she belong to?" I choked out my questions slowly, one at a time, mouth still full of blood and vomit.

"She is ours, love." Alexander put my naked body in to the bath.

I hated to admit how good the water felt against my aching muscles. "What do you mean ours? She said she came from the Underworld." I tried to sit with my body scrunched together. My brother already had enough of a show.

"Two hundred years ago, you gave birth to our daughter- mine and Baht's. She lived until she was six years old. She was marvelous. She was fragile. Cassius found us. He tried to take you back. I don't think he meant to, he's disgustingly too good of a person for that. He killed Ophelia. Baht couldn't take it. She tried to kill herself so she could go to the Underworld to be with our daughter. You were the one who stayed Baht's hand. She was so frail and you took over. I have no idea what happened to you after that." Alexander was washing my body with a loofah.

I didn't know if I was shuddering from his touch or his story. Ophelia's death was not one Adam had told me about during our last night together.

Ophelia came back into the bathroom carrying a bathrobe. She had changed out of her bloody clothes but she had not bathed. She still had blood on her neck and in her hair. "Daddy brought me back from the Underworld to be with my mommy again." Ophelia's face grew dark. "You aren't my mommy. I want her back!" Ophelia began screaming at the top of her lungs.

Alexander held her letting Ophelia scream into his chest. For someone so evil he was actually a decent father. Of course his daughter was also evil. That evil had come out of me. I had made that evil and brought it into this world. I had to stop this. I couldn't let them continue to exist.

I stood up in the bathtub using Alexander as support to climb out. There weren't any weapons or household items I could use as weapons. I put the bathrobe on. When I was tying it I realized I could use the robe's sash as a garrote. I slipped the sash around Alexander's neck pulling it as tightly as I could. He struggled to breath against the fabric at his throat. Ophelia screamed and tried to help him. Alexander's body went slack. I let it drop to the floor. I hesitated before making a move toward Ophelia. I knew I had to kill her too. As evil as she was, she was still just a little girl.

I could feel water all around me. Why was I feeling water? I wasn't in the bathtub anymore. I blinked. I was still in the bathtub. None of that had happened? Alexander was still bathing me. Ophelia wasn't even in the room.

I heard a voice laugh inside of my head. Baht was toying with me now. She was stronger than I was. She was allowing me to be present for this because she knew how much knowing what happed to me when my soul was dormant would torment me for eternity.

What was I going to do?

Chapter 7

I was slow to wake. I rolled over on my side to get closer to Adam who I could hear breathing next to me. I opened my eyes to watch Adam sleep for a few minutes before I went back to sleep. It wasn't Adam lying next to me. Alexander was lying next to me. We were both naked. The events of I didn't remember being with him after my bath. I couldn't decide if Baht was sparing me from the events of last night or trying to torture me more by making sure I didn't know exactly what I did with my own body. I rolled over to look at the clock on the bedside table. Midnight. Another day had gone by without my mind being present.

This was a one room cabin. Where was Ophelia? Did she watch us do whatever it was that we did while we were in bed naked? I sat up covering myself with the thin sheets from the bed.

Alexander rolled over staring at me from his position on his back. He didn't bother to reposition the sheets to cover himself. I guess it wasn't anything I hadn't already seen. "Ophelia isn't here, Selene. She spends most nights hunting."

"Hunting? She's six!" Why was I so indignant about the nighttime habits of an evil child that was not mine?

"She's actually two hundred and six. She can take care of herself." Alexander rolled over to go back to sleep. I saw the tattoo of the closed Eye of Horus on Alexander's back.

I heard wolves howl in the distance. Alexander and I bolted upright at the same time. My salvation may have just come in the form of a pack of wolves. I was the goddess of the moon right? All wolves answered to me. Let's hope it wasn't just werewolves with human minds but all types of canines.

I wanted to get out of bed and get dressed. Alexander was still in the room. It wasn't like he hadn't seen and defiled my naked body before. This time I wanted it to be my choice if he saw me naked or not. I was definitely making the choice for him to not see me naked any more than Baht forced me.

The cabin door blew out of the frame with the force of a stick of dynamite behind it. Not dynamite. Adam. It took him a second to register Alexander and me in the bed. Naked. It took me even longer to realize I might have some explaining to do if Adam let us both live.

Anubis came in carrying Ophelia. She was either unconscious or playing dead again. Anubis set Ophelia down on the kitchen table. She opened her eyes and winked at me.

"Anubis, look out!" I screamed for Anubis. It was too late.

Ophelia grabbed Anubis's sacred dagger from his belt. He kept trying to move toward her. She was using the dagger to lash out at him. She was considerable shorter and faster than Anubis. He was having a hard time blocking her attacks and getting close enough to attack her back. Anubis had cuts along his forearms. His blood was dripping all over the kitchen floor. It was kind of mesmerizing watching each blood droplet pool on his arm then slowly free-fall through the air until it met the floor with a force so great the droplet was flattened by gravity and physics.

Adam was a better warrior than I was. He registered Anubis but left the man to fight his own battles. A motley crew of enforcers from Vampireville trailed in- a couple of vampires, a handful of werewolves, a banshee. What? Why was Sylvia here? Banshees were only good for one thing and it wasn't fighting. Banshees predicted deaths.

Adam had Alexander by the throat against the headboard. All of Alexander was showing. I averted my eyes. It was probably something I had seen before when Baht was in my body. She wasn't here, I was and I didn't really want to see my long lost brother's naked body more than I had to.

I slipped out of bed taking the entire sheet with me. I didn't see any clothes lying around Alexander and Baht's seedy house of horrors so I wrapped the sheet around me tying it at the top like a toga. It would have to do. I didn't want to get in between my husband and my part time lover. Their battle had moved from the bed, through a hole in the wall where the window used to be, to the front lawn.

I slipped to the side of Ophelia and kneed her in the face. She shrieked like the devil was coming out of her. Too bad I couldn't actually cure her by knocking the devil out of her. I knew no amount of punishment would stop her from implementing all of the bad habits her parents had taught her. When I broke her nose, Ophelia dropped the dagger. Anubis had it in his hands now. He was just as hesitant as I was to kill a child no matter the breadth of the child's malevolent energy. I wrenched the dagger from Anubis's hand knowing what I had to do.

I took a deep breath and held it as I used Anubis's dagger to stab Ophelia in the heart. This time, the blood seeping out onto her dress was her own. This time, she was not playing a trick on me. This time, she would not get up.

My entire body was shaking. I could hear a woman screaming. I was the only woman in the room except for Sylvia. Her mouth was closed. The screaming in my brain died down to reveal my own voice screaming at my loss, just one more in a long line for me. I was so numb from everything that I shut down. I couldn't turn off my feelings like a faucet and I just over-flowed with emotions.

I was actually screaming not Baht, though I'm sure somewhere in the deep recesses of my mind she was there. I was also sure that a piece of her had died when I killed Ophelia. I know a piece of my soul ferried that little girl to the Underworld and I would never get it back. Even though I was the one who had to kill her before she destroyed the rest of the world, Ophelia's death hit me like a bullet. Only this time I

69

wasn't going to wake up a couple of hours later like nothing had ever happened. This death was my fault and I would always carry the burden of this loss with me like an albatross around my neck.

I faintly heard Adam in the background of my life giving orders to the Asylum personnel scattered about the cabin and its grounds. "Alexander escaped. Find him."

"It is done." Sylvia glanced at me briefly, her eyes devoid of all sentiment, before she walked outside.

The only death Sylvia could never predict was the death of her emotions. When all you see is death day in and day out, you stop caring about people you might have to see die one day. The only reason why she was here was to see her prediction come true. She was the type of person who liked to be right all of the time. She liked to go out with the strike teams and see if her predictions came true or not. In all the time I've known her, she has never been wrong.

"Sylvia predicted one death today." Adam whispered in my hair from behind me putting his arms around my waist. "I'm sorry I couldn't spare you from having to kill her. When I killed Ophelia two hundred years ago I thought she would stay dead."

"Even though she might have been our daughter? Mine and yours?" I peered up at him through the water that had begun pooling in my eyes.

"I had hoped that I would find you both and we could start our life over together. When I found you, you told me your mom was right and you had married Alexander. Ophelia tried to kill me. Something wasn't right about her. I just- I," Adam didn't go on. He couldn't.

I wrapped my arms around his waist. "None of that was me. It was all Baht."

"I wish I would have known that at the time. I killed Ophelia, then I left. I left you. It was the worst moment of my life. I have been looking for you ever since. I promise will never leave your side again." Adam buried his face in my hair.

"Alexander used the *Book of the Dead* to bring Ophelia's soul back from the Underworld. You couldn't have known he had the book or what he was going to do with it." Tears fell from my eyes at a slower velocity than before. I ruminated on what I had just said. Alexander had used the *Book of the Dead*. That meant he still had it, right? It couldn't be here, could it?

Adam held me tighter to his chest until the tears stopped completely.

I pushed back from him. "How did you guys find me?"

Adam's anger started to build until it rolled off of him like fog coming in with the tide.

I had said something to set him off. I wasn't sure what it was. I hadn't left him on purpose. Surely, he knew that?

Adam blew a puff of air out of his mouth above my head. "Baht didn't leave a trail of clues to follow when she took over your body and spirited you away from Asylum. You're lucky a full moon came up or I don't think we ever would have been able to find you."

That explained all of the howling we heard before the frame of the cabin rocked off of its foundation when Adam came in to rescue me. That did not explain why he was so cheesed off. I had a terrible thought that maybe he thought I wanted to be here with Alexander. Since I couldn't just brush the thought away like a fly on a hot summer day, I decided to see if that was Adam's problem.

I put my hands back on his chest partially to feel the warmth of his body in my soul and partially to keep us both steady so whatever this was wouldn't develop into something beyond saving. "You said it yourself, Baht brought me here. You know I didn't choose this, choose to leave you, right?"

I had a hard time looking him in the eyes. His stare was making me feel like it *had* been my choice to leave him in the first place.

Adam stepped away from my hands. They grazed his shirt as they fell. Adam shuddered.

"It wasn't that Alexander and you were together. I know that wasn't your choice." Adam sighed and ran his hands through his hair. I could tell he was having a hard time finding the right words. "It was that when I found you, *you* and Alexander were together. *You* were in control of your body and *you* weren't resisting him. When I walked in, after looking for you for *three* days, you seemed content to just be there with him not come home. To me."

So it was jealousy that was driving this little temper tantrum? Whether I was myself (whoever that was) or Baht, I would never understand men. There was no reason to be jealous. Was there? No. Definitely not. I was with Adam not Alexander. Even if I could get over the fact that Alexander was my *brother*, his brand of crazy was not something I was attracted to. Attracted to killing maybe. Not dating.

I didn't know what to say. It bothered me too that I had just sat there and let someone else rescue me. It bothered me too that I couldn't blame that complacency on Baht. It bothered me too that I wasn't more upset by finding myself in Alexander's bed. I had resigned myself to my fate just then. I never once thought I could be the one to change my own future. Maybe it wasn't my future I needed to change. Maybe it was my past.

"I love you. I know you know that. I also know I don't tell you that often enough. Don't worry. I will fix this. I will fix us." I kissed Adam with everything I had left.

The kiss was fire and tongue and a passion I never knew I was capable of. I had to leave him to save him. To save us. He was all I had left in this world. I wanted to be able to take him to the next with me. I wanted to be able to never let him go. I couldn't do that if I was constantly worried about him or his feelings while I was trying to kill my brother and his evil wife. I couldn't take Adam into a fight with my mother knowing her end game was to destroy us both along with the rest of the world. I couldn't knowingly and willingly endanger his life. I would have to find some way to leave him that would still let him forgive me one day. I wanted to be with him. Just not today, not until the world was safe to love again.

72

I remembered something he told me on our wedding night. I don't know what made me think of it just then. I knew he needed to hear it now. "If you've got eternity, so do I."

He smiled. He remembered his promise to me all those millennia ago.

I smiled back when I remembered the *Book of the Dead* didn't just have spells to ferry souls to the Afterlife. It had spells for other things, things like making people forget. I had to get my hands on that book.

I used Adam's shoulder to balance on a kitchen chair and become the goddess I was born to be. "Listen up, Alexander has been using the *Book of the Dead* to bring souls back from the Underworld. Start a grid search on this entire property inside and out. Find me that book."

I got down from the chair turning to Adam. A look of concern shadowed the features of his face like he could read my mind and knew *exactly* why I needed that book. He frowned at me. Adam went to the other side of the cabin to search for the book or pretend he was searching for the book. I wasn't really all that sure. One thing I was sure of though. Our marriage would be in real trouble if I couldn't stop sleeping with my brother.

Chapter 8

We didn't find the book. I had a dozen trained men comb through every inch of that woodland property. We didn't find anything useful. In fact, it looked like Alexander and Ophelia didn't even really live there. It looked like a summer cottage with a few necessities not a full time residence.

The only thing I did find was that maybe Adam and I no longer knew each other as well as we thought. Maybe all of this emotional and mental dissonance created by Baht taking over my body whenever it suited her was taking a real toll on our relationship. Maybe because of all that had happened to us we didn't know ourselves that well so we couldn't expect the other to figure it out. None of that was either of our faults. Neither of us could stop what was happening either.

"Come on," I grabbed Adam's hand pulling him behind me.

He didn't resist but he did question the hell out of me. Good to see that no matter how much we were changing as people and how different we were as a married couple now as opposed to several hundred years ago, some things would never truly change.

"Where are we going?"

"To the file room." I shouted giving my forefinger an upward thrust.

"You know, in all of our time together, I don't think we have ever made love in a file room."

I laughed. "I wasn't planning on making love to anyone down there. I was actually planning on retrieving a file so we could see what Asylum had on all of our players. Now that you mention it, I think you're right. I don't think we have ever been together in a file room." I winked pulling Adam closer.

"I don't think today should be the day you break your all-time love making record."

Adam and I both jumped. James. Man, I hated that guy. He ruined everything.

James narrowed his eyes at us. He knew we were up to something he couldn't prove. Yet. Reginald came up to James and handed him a clip-board and a pen. James frowned and began flipping through the papers attached to the clip-board. Adam and I took that opportunity to sneak off to the file room.

We were stopped by Reginald blocking our path. We looked behind us where James was still standing down the hall flipping through paperwork. Reggie wasn't next to James anymore because he was here, in front of us. He was a swift little bugger. I was just opening my mouth to ask him where he had been and what the other griffins said when he cut me off.

"I have found a woman who may have the information you were looking for." Reginald handed me a slip of paper before darting off in the opposite direction. I guess I would have to ask him later how his family reunion went.

I shrugged at Adam. After spending three days with Alexander and no memory of what had happened, having Reginald hand me a slip of paper and walking away was no big deal.

I unfolded the paper while we walked to the file room. I still wanted to see what Asylum knew about Alexander before I faced him again. I also wanted to see if they knew where the *Book of the Dead* was. I would kill at least half a dozen people if I found out the book had been in our library this whole time.

I unfolded the scrap of paper Reggie had thrust upon me like the responsibility James had thrust upon me when he offered me the job last year. The slip of paper had one word written in Reginald's neat, clean handwriting.

Cosmescu

The only Cosmescu I knew was a cheap old world fortune teller. Madame Cosmescu was well known in the supernatural circles that I travelled. She wasn't a fraud by any means but she frequently committed fraudulent acts towards humans- mostly on the wedding circuit. I'd warned her a few times about it. We both knew there was nothing I could do since she wasn't technically breaking any of the Laws of the Covenant that Asylum had put into place to protect the things that go bump in the night from the prying eyes of the world.

If this was all Reggie gave me she must have been in the files. Shame some things weren't digitized around here, like the files. It's not like there weren't a ton of vamps hanging around who could take the time to scan them to a digital database. James didn't think it was secure. I bet he's just messing with me and all of the files are digitized and I couldn't have access because he's an asshole. Maybe it was a good thing the files weren't just something I could look up in three seconds on a computer. It meant that Adam and I had more alone time together. Bonus that it was a place we had never been together before.

There were at least three people actively filing papers when we walked in. So much for checking file room off our bucket list. I went over to the C's now that I knew what we were looking for.

Let's see- Claybourne. He was dead now. I killed him last year when he wolfed out in the middle of the Founder's Day parade. Come to think of it I still don't know what set him off. I made a mental note to re-open his case when I was done killing Alexander.

Copperbolt. He was the vampire who tried to eat me and destroy traditional paper news. James got that one for me. Or, probably his strike team. Didn't matter, he was dead.

I rifled through a few other deceased members of society before I found what we were looking for.

Cosmescu.

"Got it!" I pulled the file out of the drawer giving myself a paper cut with the file folder. "Damn."

"Let me see," Adam closed the slight gap of air between us in the span of a heartbeat.

I handed him the file folder. He didn't take it. Instead, he grabbed my bleeding finger and put it in his mouth.

I grinned and took possession of my finger back so I could look at the file. "She lives in the city. Last known address 12th and Demonbreun. It would be a drive but we could road trip it." I closed the file to put it back in the cabinet when something fell out.

Adam picked it up. It was a picture of Mitch. My biggest demon fan Mitch. Weird for a picture of him to be in a file for Madame Cosmescu.

I took the picture from Adam and flipped it over. Mitch Cosmescu? That's not what his name tag said. Was it? Did I even care in that moment when I met Mitch to read his nametag? I don't think I did. Hell, I couldn't even remember if he had been wearing a name tag or just a white lab coat.

I opened the file back up to see what it said about Mitch. Nothing. It was just a picture attached to the file that referred to Mitch's file. I put the picture back in Madame Cosmescu's file. I re-filed the reports we had on her and pulled Mitch's file out.

"Why are we so interested in this guy? I thought it was the old lady we needed to see." Adam took Mitch's file from me and flipped through it.

I grabbed the file back from him so I could see for myself. "He is the medical examiner's assistant who tried to kill me. I'm just interested in seeing what Asylum knew about him before he tried to kill me."

Mitch Cosmescu, twenty-three, no known aliases, next of kin Madame Luiza Cosmescu, known associates Alexander Helios.

I dropped the file scattering the papers all over the floor of the file room. Adam picked up the papers shoveling them back into the file folder in no particular order. He crammed the file back in the cabinet slamming the drawer as hard as he could. I heard the metal cabinet give way under the pressure of his touch.

"Mitch worked for Alexander. Asylum has known about Alexander all this time. Who did they think Alexander was? Some low level criminal?" My hands ran through my hair making it stick up in the back.

Adam looked like he would rather be making a mess out of the file room. He was just as resigned to this job as I was. We both knew we couldn't move on with our lives until we had dealt with our shared past in some kind of way.

I searched another filing cabinet containing the letter H for Alexander's file. It wasn't there. Asylum had to have a file on him even if it was just a list of known aliases.

"Nothing on Alexander. Let me see if they have anything on Cleopatra." I searched through the C's and didn't find anything. I also looked through the P's since my mother's full name was Cleopatra VII Thea Philopator.

"Nothing on either of them! This is James's fault, he's totally fucking with us." I bit my lower lip.

I didn't know how to find my mother. I didn't know how to find my brother unless I let Baht take over my body again. I didn't know how to get Baht's soul out of my body. I felt useless and hopeless. The only thing I could think to do was find Madame Cosmescu and find out what she knew since Reggie thought she was a good lead.

Adam gave me an agonized look. I hadn't even noticed how close he was, how he was pressing my body against the file cabinets with his. I looked up at him. I'll admit it. I am a terrible person. I knew

79

exactly what I was doing when I did it, but I did it anyway. I bit my lower lip again. It didn't take Adam long to respond with his body.

Fireworks went off in every neuron of my body every time he touched me. It was an unnatural response even to someone you loved. I didn't care. We didn't care. All that mattered was that we were together.

We heard a cough and remembered there had been other people in the file room when we came in. I relied on Adam's height to confirm whether we were alone or if we had an audience. Adam didn't see anyone over the file cabinets. He shrugged.

"I apologize for interrupting you, my lady." Anubis was behind Adam who was blocking my view of the rest of the file room. Anubis was looking everywhere except at us.

To be fair we had most of our clothes off.

"I'm betting you aren't regretting interrupting us more than we are." I struggled to reach my blouse off the top of one of the file cabinets.

Adam handed it to me. "Why *are* you interrupting us, Anubis?"

"A body was just brought in by Sheriff Larry. There was some type of attack at the morgue. Sheriff thinks it looks demonic in origin, with Alexander on the loose he didn't want to take any chances." Anubis still wasn't looking in our direction.

"What are you leaving out?" Adam shifted his eyes from my half-naked body to Anubis.

"The body is Sylvia. We aren't sure why she was at the morgue or what she was investigating." Anubis was still concentrating on a dirty tile on the floor.

"No!" I hurried too much in my attempt to dress.

I didn't even bother to put my bra back on. I just stuffed it in the back pocket of my jeans. I put my t-shirt on inside out and started for the Asylum morgue. I stopped at the file room door to let the boys catch up.

Anubis had one job in the Underworld- to ferry souls from the plane of living existence to their final resting place in the Underworld. With him here, who would ferry Sylvia to rest?

The one good thing about Asylum was the fact that it was completely self-sustaining. In the advent of some kind of zombie apocalypse any and all supernatural creatures (except for zombies- no one likes those guys) could live out their days here. We didn't expect a zombie apocalypse any time soon. Zombies aren't exactly known for their cunning and planning skills. They would never be able to pull off a world ending event. Vampires maybe. They lived forever and they were dicks about everything. Hanging out with vampires was like being on a reality television show called cranky old men and the things they complain about.

Asylum had its own morgue. Someone had the forethought to install it so we could find out how our own died. The only time having our own morgue was actually useful was in 1852 when new wolves kept dying after their first full moon. Some insect whose bite only affected canines was prevalent at the time. New wolves are now vaccinated when discovered. Go figure even supernatural beings needed vaccinations like the rest of us.

I sprinted down the corridor of one of the basement levels to the morgue. I had to see for myself if Sylvia died because of me or if her death was coincidental and unrelated to everything going on with Alexander. In my line of work though, there was no such thing as a coincidence.

I swung open one set of double doors leading into the morgue. I stopped short of the other set. I didn't want to see Sylvia on the morgue table. Despite her inability to smile, I actually liked her and considered her a friend. I could never tell if she shared the sentiment. That didn't matter too much to me. I didn't really have any other friends, especially none I could spare to stainless steel tables and blunt blades that cut rough lines into flesh.

Adam hugged me from behind. "I'm right here," he whispered in my ear.

I took a deep breath holding it until I was through the second set of doors and I heard them whoosh closed behind me.

"Hey, Sebastian, what's the word on this one?" I waved at our medical examiner, a nachzehrer (which is a sort of vampire and ghoul hybrid).

Sebastian took after his mother, a vampire. The only truly ghoulish quality he had was that he was a huge creep who hit on anything that moved.

"Selene, you are looking lovely as usual." Sebastian stepped closer.

He was a hand kisser all the way.

I normally tolerated it because any time I came down to the morgue I needed information. Letting Sebastian kiss my hand was the only way I could get it. Adam, however, was not tolerant of much these days. He stepped between me and Sebastian before Sebastian could soak the back of my hand with his saliva.

Sebastian was not pleased. I could tell by the way he told me about Sylvia's body. "She's got Sulphur all over her which normally only happens during a demon attack. However, these marks here," Sebastian used a scalpel to point to Sylvia's bare torso, "and here," and to her forearms, "suggest knife work. Skilled knife work to be sure. I mistook these marks for demon scratches at first."

"What made you change your mind?" Adam was more interested in Sylvia's wounds than I was in looking at her corpse.

I turned away from the autopsy table. How many people had to die because of me? How many had died before Sylvia? Should I count all of the people I killed or just the ones that I couldn't save? I should have been able to save Sylvia. I should have known Alexander would do something like this, something to hurt me. If I could ever truly say I had a best friend, it would be Sylvia hands down. I had lost one of the pieces in the foundation of who I was and I would never get it back.

"No Sulphur inside of the wounds. It was almost as if the Sulphur was sprinkled on the body after the fact." Sebastian took off his gloves and picked up a raw cheeseburger.

I guess it was feeding time at the petting zoo.

I glanced over at Sylvia's body one more time. "Anubis, what are you doing?"

Anubis was sniffing Sylvia's body. His mouth said nothing. his face said there was something about this kill that he recognized.

"Anubis, come on. Don't make me order you to tell me what you know." I put my hands on my hips, waiting. I hated waiting. I may have mentioned that before.

"Ammut, mistress. I think Ammut did this." Anubis hung his head.

"Who is Ammut?" Adam put his hand on Anubis's shoulder.

"My mate." Anubis's words hung in the air until they grew stale.

We all knew why Ammut's scent was all over Sylvia's body. Ammut had killed her and covered it up to look like a demon attack. What we didn't know was why. Was she working for Alexander or was she a free agent?

I sighed. Life just got a hell of a lot more complicated. "We should go see if Madame Cosmescu is alive, I guess. If Alexander and Ammut are picking off people who might have information on them, there's no telling who's next."

I hated to say it. I actually liked Madame Cosmescu, the old bag. We always had pleasant exchanges, weird, but pleasant. I hoped she was a good enough fortune teller to predict the possibility of Ammut coming for her. Maybe I was wrong. I was hoping I was wrong.

It hadn't worked out that well for Sylvia. Unless she had predicted her own death and went to the morgue to see if she was

83

right. I doubted it. It was more likely that she found some information she didn't want to share until she knew she was right.

When Sylvia wasn't in the field watching the deaths she predicted, she worked as an intake officer. She hadn't been in the field in any official capacity when she died. Something about her last intake must have warranted her visit the morgue. Until we found out what she knew, we would be at a disadvantage. It seemed like Alexander was attempting to take away my sources of information.

I stomped through both sets of double doors until I was out in the hall. Reggie was there.

"Selene, I need to talk to you." Reggie grabbed my arm pulling me away from Adam and Anubis who were coming out of the last set of morgue doors.

"Reggie, glad you're here. I need you to find out who Sylvia's last intake was. They may be the reason why Sylvia is dead now." I pushed Reggie's hand off my arm. I wasn't in the mood to be a pleasant person anymore today.

"We already looked into that. She did an intake on a new vamp who didn't survive the process of turning. He's probably somewhere in the morgue too. We have no idea why Sylvia was at the city morgue. Our only thought is that she was lured there somehow. We have the tech team pouring through her phone and computer." Reggie paused to take a breath before continuing. "I spoke with the last remaining griffins. While they agree that your mother must be stopped, they will not help us. They fear their numbers are too low already and will not sacrifice their race for your war."

"Fine. I didn't expect them to." I pushed off of the wall I had been leaning on listening to Reggie deliver bad news on top of bad news. I motioned to Adam and Anubis making a circle in the air with my finger. "Let's move out."

Chapter 9

We arrived at Madame Cosmescu's last known address during full night. All of the lights in her house were on unlike any other house in her subdivision. The front door was open. I didn't want to enter the brick ranch style house. I looked at Adam. He shook his head. We were in agreement on that at least. Neither of us wanted to see the horrors that house had to offer. Anubis was already on the porch sniffing the air and frowning. Ammut must have been here recently.

Adam and I followed Anubis up the front porch steps. We took a deep breath and walked in the house together. We could hear Anubis searching the house room by room. The place had been trashed. That much was evident from the second we walked in.

The front entryway had a small table under a mirror. The operative word here being had. Pieces of the mirror crunched under our feet as we stepped all the way into the house. The table lay broken into a weird jig-saw puzzle. The ornamental rug was scrunched to one side of the hall. Someone had been dragged through here.

Anubis came around the corner from a side room. "Ammut is not here. I found the fortune teller though."

We followed Anubis through the small house. Before she had Ammut as a house guest, Madame Cosmescu kept a clean and organized home. Despite all of her belongings lying broken on the floors of every room, I could tell everything lying there had a place where it was normally kept. There were no traces of dust or cobwebs.

86

I stooped down to pick up a religious figurine that had fallen to the floor during the commotion of whatever had happened here. The saint depicted in porcelain was unharmed. He must have been the saint of violent deaths. I set him down gently on a credenza shelf. He seemed like he belonged there. A feeling of peace washed over me.

We found Madame Cosmescu in the kitchen. She had the same knife wounds and Sulphur sprinkled on her as Sylvia. I knelt beside her stroking her hair trying to comfort myself. Another person had died for a reason directly related to me. At this rate, I would never find out what kind of revolution the tattoo of the closed Eye of Horus foretold or how I was going to get Baht's soul out of my body.

Madame Cosmescu gnarled, arthritic hand reached out and grabbed my wrist. I startled. I didn't expect her to still be alive.

I removed her hand from my wrist and held it. "Get me some towels. She's still alive."

Adam opened all of the drawers in the kitchen that weren't already torn from their tracks until he found some hand towels. He handed all of them to me. I tied a few around her forearms to staunch the bleeding there while I pressed the rest of them to her chest.

"Copilul meu, Selene. It's too late for me, not for you. I left your birthday gift under the floorboards of your room." Madame Cosmescu closed her eyes.

I had no idea what she was talking about. I didn't have a room here and it was nowhere near my birthday.

Adam checked her pulse and shook his head. "She's gone, Selene. What do you want to do now?"

"Check under the floorboards in every room. Look for anything that could be misconstrued as a present. Anything in a box, wrapped or not, anything in a bag, just anything."

The boys had their marching orders. I stayed with Madame Cosmescu. I didn't want to leave her so soon. She was a hack and a con artist but she didn't deserve to die this way. She was just one more on a long list of people who died because of me. Every time someone died because of me another piece of my soul left my body. At this rate, none of me would be left in my body. By next week, Baht could do whatever she wanted with it.

I could hear Adam and Anubis ripping up planks of wood floor in every room of the house. They came back empty handed. I leaned back against her retro white kitchen cabinets trying to think. We couldn't leave her here alone. I texted Asylum. They would send someone to clean up the house and make it look like she had moved into a nursing home or something so the general human public wouldn't get suspicious.

"The only room I have, or had, other than the one at Vampireville, is the one at my old apartment, the one I had lived in before I died the first time. You don't think she hid something there because she knew someone would come for her, do you?" I looked at the boys hoping one of them would have a bright idea. They said nothing confirming for me girls really were smarter than boys.

I closed Madame Cosmescu's eyes and placed her hands over her chest. It would be another forty-five minutes or so before anyone from Asylum would be here to clean up this mess. I stood at the sink washing her blood from my hands lost in thought. My life didn't add up. There was still so much that I was missing that I had to get back somehow.

Adam touched my shoulder like he was touching me for the first time. "Let's go. There's nothing more we can do here."

I turned the faucet off and reached for a towel. I had used them all in my futile attempt to save Madame Cosmescu's life. I shook my hands out in the sink and wiped the remaining water droplets on the back of my jeans.

We left Madame Cosmescu's house turning off lights as we walked through. We closed the front door leaving her behind.

Chapter 10

Being back at my old apartment was like meeting an old friend. I didn't know why I ever left. Oh, yeah, because I died. Being dead took the fun out of everything. I tried the door. Unlocked. I hoped I wasn't walking in on some unsuspecting family who just forgot to lock their door. Then again, part of me was a little bit of a jerk who would have loved to scare the crap out of some kids using my space even though it wasn't my space anymore. It hadn't been mine in a long time. I also don't think this building had been inhabited in a long time. I still would have liked to scare some people just because.

No one was in there. The apartment was still just as empty as it had been the night of my first death. I guess I have to stop calling it that- my "first" death. My first death had been with Cleopatra two millennia ago. Maybe it didn't count as a death because my soul never left my body. That would make my poor attempt at being vampire chow my first official death then. Right? Ugh, I hate being undead. There were too many questions left unanswered with no one to answer them.

I strode through the empty apartment to my old bedroom. My old apartment was in the same abandoned apartment building Adam and Anubis had brought me to after the hellhound fight in the alley behind *The Tipsy Cow*. It looked completely different without my things in there. I looked out of window. We were two floors up from the apartment Adam had chosen to bring me to. It felt like a hundred years had passed since the night Adam came back into my life.

I couldn't stand at the window to my past reminiscing forever. I had to find what Madame Cosmescu left for me. I walked along the baseboards first, looking for anything out of the ordinary. I didn't see anything. Madame Cosmescu hadn't written me any notes on the walls or left any x's marking the spot where she hid what I needed to know. Short of gutting the room like we had at her house, I wasn't sure we were going to find what we were looking for. To be honest, I wasn't sure there was actually anything to find. A dying woman's words couldn't necessarily be trusted. Especially if she was a professional liar for a living.

I was about to give the order to tear the place apart floorboard by floorboard when something caught my eye. A light shimmered under an upside down floorboard in the center of the room. When I went to pry up the floorboard I noticed the Eye of Horus had been hastily carved into the wood. This was not the closed eye like the tattoos on Mitch and my mother. This was the eye drawn correctly. This open eye meant protection of royalty. I still had no idea what the closed eye actually stood for, no idea what my mother meant when she began using it for her little revolution. If I had to guess I would say it was the mark of someone out to get royalty or who didn't recognize royalty. It sort of seemed to mean the opposite of the open eye. Madame Cosmescu had left me a sign after all. I greedily pushed the floorboard aside and snatched the vial hidden underneath.

I stared at the pretty glass bottle beveled with a flower pattern, the pink liquid swirling inside even though my hands were still. I was mesmerized by the possibility and I didn't even know why the fortune teller wanted me to have this potion. I didn't even know what the potion did. There was a note attached. I untied the ribbon unfurling a scrap of parchment. Great. It was more cryptic gypsy bullshit. Has this woman never heard of giving it to people straight?

Drink if you want your life to be your own

I turned the small slip of paper over and over in my hands. I held it up to the light to see if there was a hidden message. Adam took the slip of paper from me and did the same thing. We weren't getting anywhere new. This was it. I needed to drink this sickly sweet looking liquid to make my life my own again.

"Bottoms up, boys." I tipped the pink liquid in my mouth to the sounds of Adam's protestations.

His points were valid. We didn't know if Madame Cosmescu was on our side or not. At this point it didn't matter. The pink liquid that had swirled in the vial without my help was now swirling inside my body. It had tasted just as disgustingly sweet as I thought it would. I hoped it would taste better on the way back up than it had going down because it felt like up was the direction the potion was taking.

I dropped to my knees. Something was wrong. Maybe I should have listened to my husband when he said not to take potions from strangers. My entire body shook. The inside of my body was so cold but my skin felt like it was blistering and flaking off. How could I freeze and burn at the same time?

As my body writhed on the floor, I could vaguely hear Adam's voice trying to bring me back from wherever I had just gone. As most things that have to do with magic go I had no idea how I ended up where I ended up or what I was supposed to do now that I was there. I knew someone who could tell me.

Baht.

I was inside of my own head talking to the one person with all of the answers. And she was pissed. She didn't miss a beat. As soon as I showed up she started screaming obscenities at me and putting her finger in my face. I don't like being called a bitch in my own mind so I punched her in the face. She took that as a declaration of war and punched me back. Soon we were testing our true abilities and proving to each other who the better warrior goddess was.

I was not about to lose this battle for my own body. A cage appeared. I didn't know if that was my doing or the potion's and I didn't care. I needed Baht to act like the caged animal she was. Since I was currently straddling her and punching her in the face repeatedly, I felt like I had the upper hand and now was the time to act. Baht flipped me over so I was on my back blocking her glancing blows. Ugh, I really have to get out of my own head more often.

I pulled my knees up as high as I could then used her torso to kick off. She landed on her feet. I scrambled to get up before she could touch me again. I skirted around her getting closer to the cage. She followed until my back hit metal. I just needed one good hit to spin her around and push her into the open door of the cage. She grabbed me by the shirt collar and spun me in the opposite direction of where we needed to be. I was starting to think I wasn't as good of a fighter as Anubis told me I used to be. Or, maybe, I just didn't have anything left to fight for.

"Stop, Baht. What are we even doing? You know you don't belong here." I held my hands up in surrender.

"I know. I didn't belong in the Underworld either. You put me there." Baht still had me by the collar. She pushed me further into the bars behind me.

"Liar! I didn't send you to the Underworld." I really didn't remember killing her and sending her to the Underworld though I wasn't sure that if I had done that I would have thought twice about it. She belonged to Alexander. If she was a typical woman who would do anything for the man that she loved like I would for Adam, then Baht deserved everything she got. Too bad she didn't see it that way.

"Selene, I'm not the one keeping that memory from you, you are. You killed me for no reason. To top it off, you didn't even mourn me. No wonder Alexander wants to find a way to kill your soul for good." Baht pushed me against the bars of the cage one more time before letting me go and stepping back from me.

Neither one of us moved for what felt like an hour. I'm sure it was only a matter of seconds. It was long enough for me to come up with another plan to deceive her.

"I'm sorry. We used to be friends and I betrayed you." I went in for a hug.

She let me. Baht had dropped her guard. I used that moment to betray her again. Even though I didn't remember betraying her in the first place, I was certain I had. Baht was an easy girl to betray being evil and all.

93

I punched her in the gut and elbowed her in the face in rapid succession. I spun around so I was behind her dragging her to the entrance of the cage by her hair. Baht kicked her legs up trying to break my grip. I dragged her into the cage behind me. Before I left the cage, I kicked her in the face as hard as I could. She was lying on the ground in the cage bleeding and I was locking the cage door behind me.

I wanted to gloat, I just couldn't. The spell Madame Cosmescu had created was wearing off. I could see my old bedroom blurring into existence then blend back into Baht in her cage, now standing and wiping blood off of her face with her bare arm. I had one shot to get the answers I needed before the spell wore off completely.

Baht had the closed Eye of Horus tattoo on her left back shoulder. Her sheer nude-colored traditional Egyptian dress was cut in such a way it looked like she didn't have a dress on at all. I had seen the tattoo during our fight.

"Baht," I moved closer to the bars of her cage, not close enough for her to grab me, "what does your tattoo mean?"

"What tattoo?" She responded dryly playing with one of the bracelets that lined the length of her arms.

"You only have the one of the closed Eye of Horus on your back. What do you mean 'what tattoo'?" I shot back anger welling up inside of me.

"Oh, that." Baht pretended to inspect her fingernails trying to play this whole conversation nonchalant. "It's not a tattoo. It's the mark of my master."

The inner workings of my mind started to fray at the edges again. I could hear Adam's voice calling me home.

"What is your master's plan?" My tongue grew thick causing me to slur my words. I was getting dizzy. "Where is your master?"

The part of my mind Baht and I both inhabited dimmed. I could see Baht smirk. She wasn't going to tell me what I wanted to know before I went back to the real world. Baht paced her new cage

94

smiling, evil filling her eyes, looking triumphant. What had she won? Not the fight we had just had, not control over my body. I would make sure she never used my body to see Alexander again. She had to know that.

I collapsed on the ground in front of the cage. I woke up on the floor of my old bedroom. Adam and Anubis were hovering like my two over-protective dads. Apparently, the whole point of the potion was for my soul to fight Baht's soul for dominance over my body. I'm just glad I won.

The drink to take back your life thing did happen. I guess if she would have written a book to explain it I wouldn't have done it? Whatever. A better warning would have been nice. I didn't know how long Baht would stay locked in my mind. I had to find a spell to get her soul out of my body. The only book I knew that probably had the spell I needed was hidden somewhere only Alexander could find it.

Chapter 11

A lot of things were bothering me about my life. At present it was the location of the *Book of the Dead* that was bothering me the most. I had to find it. The last person I knew of who had the book in his possession was Victor Frankenstein. Adam had said when he woke up Victor was dead and the book was gone. That didn't mean Victor didn't know what happened to the book or that his death wasn't directly related to the book itself.

I went looking for Anubis. If anyone could help me pull off my insane plan it would be him. I found Anubis in the cafeteria eating raw steak and what looked like dog food. I did not want to know.

"Anubis, let's say, theoretically of course, if I wanted to go to the Underworld to talk to someone could I?" I was trying to stare at Anubis's amber eyes not the piece of meat dangling from his mouth.

Anubis wiped his mouth on his sleeve. Do not get between a werewolf and their dinner and don't expect them to have any manners about it.

"No." Anubis looked at me briefly then went back to his dinner.

"What do you mean no? How do you talk to people who are dead?" I was shouting in the cafeteria. James was in there ordering a coffee. His look told me to sit down and shut up fast.

I sat back down. "Anubis, seriously, you have to do whatever I say and I need you to take me to the Underworld to talk to Victor. He's the only lead I have on the *Book of the Dead.* Don't you want to take it back to Osiris?" I put my hand on his. It felt weird. I wasn't really a touchy feely kind of gal.

I must never have tried to comfort him because he took hand from under mine. "The best way to contact Victor is to not. I'm sorry." Anubis looked behind me before taking his tray to the trash.

I looked behind me. James again. What was his deal? James left the cafeteria, sans coffee. I followed. I was trying to be stealth which proves difficult when everyone knows your name and says hi to you in the halls. I had just finished saying hi to a gargoyle named Ruth when James turned around making me run into him.

"James, I didn't see you there." I was trying to play it cool. I wasn't.

"Selene, I believe Anubis has given you his answer. Anubis cannot ferry you to the Underworld unless you are dead. Go see if Reginald has a case for you to work. It makes me unhappy when you don't have anything to do and are underfoot all of the time." James walked into his office and closed the door.

I didn't bother to follow. I had a better idea.

This time I would need Adam's help. He would also say no but I knew of ways to get him to agree. I found him in our living quarters cooking dinner. If I ever had doubts about loving him they were gone when I saw him in a pink apron covered in hearts and ruffles. It was the apron I got for Valentine's Day three years ago. The same one I got stood up in by my ex when he got back together with his ex. Good thing I wasn't with that loser. I would be knocked up six ways to Sunday and barefoot in a kitchen somewhere. Not my idea of a life.

"Adam, I could really use your help with something." I went into the kitchen hugging Adam from behind.

"Anubis already told me what you wanted. The answer is no. I will not ferry you back and forth from the Underworld. Good idea though. Victor would have been a great lead. Too bad the medium is dead." Adam didn't even look at me pouting next to him. He just kept stirring tomato sauce on the stovetop.

I pulled away from him. "Actually smart ass, I just need you to watch over my body after I have killed myself so I can get Anubis to ferry me to the Underworld and find Victor while still following all of his dumb rules." I put my hands on my hips. I thought this plan was genius.

Adam turned around sharply still holding the spoon he had been using to stir the sauce. Spaghetti sauce splattered across my face. His look told me while my idea was actually quite genius, he wouldn't stand by and watch me die. Not again.

I got where he was coming from. I didn't want to watch him die again either. Especially now that we didn't have the *Book of the Dead* to bring him back.

Adam handed me a dish towel. I wiped off my face. I pleaded with him through the towel, "Adam you know I'm the only one who can come back. I have to do this. Victor can help us. I don't know of any other way."

Adam moved the towel from my face. I had been using it to hide my almost tears. I was getting unnecessarily emotional. I would give myself a break. This time. It had been a rough week.

"I know. I'm not saying it's a bad idea, just that I wish there was a better one." Adam kissed me. I turned the burners on the cook top off. There would be no Underworld and no spaghetti for either of us tonight.

Chapter 12

"I do not like this mistress," Anubis was wringing his hands and fretting about the room. If I couldn't tell he didn't like this by the worry his hands created in the air like mini cyclones, I would have wondered when he reverted back to calling me mistress.

"Any way to call ahead so Victor is ready to talk to us?" I was officially kidding but also hoping there may be a chance.

"No, mistress." Anubis stopped wringing his hands but kept pacing the length of the room.

Adam and I had talked about it last night in between other activities. I was going to take a drug that made my body mimic death. The drug was designed to slow my heart to one beat per minute and paralyze my body. We thought this would be better than actually dying to give Baht less of a chance of taking over my body. We weren't sure if I died if Madame Cosmescu's potion would hold.

I laid on the kitchen table Adam and I had cleaned off in a hurry last night. I noticed a piece of broken plate and an errant fork on the carpet under the table. I would have to remember to clean that up later. James was present for our little show. He didn't say anything. He just leaned against the refrigerator watching. I noticed a magnet at his feet. Something else for me to clean up later. Adam and I really shouldn't have nice things.

"Are you ready?" Adam laid me on the table a little softer than he had last night.

"Ready." I squeezed his hand.

He leaned down to kiss me. I raised my head off the table to meet him. James cleared his throat. Adam and I broke free from each other. Anubis rolled his eyes. It was getting to be a real comedy show around here.

James took the vial of the paralysis drug from Adam's shaking hands. He skillfully used a needle to fill a syringe and inject me with the drug.

Nothing happened. I could see James and Adam standing over my body. I could feel Anubis's hand in mine. Wait. What? James and Adam were standing over my body. I was looking at my body. It had worked.

I needed confirmation. I looked to Anubis. Instead of looking like a man, he had the head of a wolf. I blinked as hard as I could. The wolf head was still there. A wolf with Anubis's eyes. "Yes, Mistress, you are dead. You may cross into the Underworld now. We cannot linger once there. It is a long and perilous journey to get back."

I felt like I was floating. I guess this was how all spirits felt since they didn't have anything to tether them to the world anymore. Anubis held my hand and did not let go until we reached an iron gate.

"Here is where you must pass the judgement of Lord Osiris. He will tell you which part of the Underworld you are allowed access to."

"So he is telling me if I should be in heaven or hell?"

"Something like that."

Anubis knocked on the gate. No one answered. The gate opened by itself.

"Strange. We normally encounter at least one of Lord Osiris's underlings by now. Let's be cautious. Alexander may have lain waste to the order of things by bringing Baht back."

My feet were touching the ground now. I wanted to go back to floating. The ground crunched under my feet. I looked down to see what I was stepping on. I shouldn't have. I was crushing the bones of skeletons that paved the walkway. What really made me sick was that all of the skeletons were alive and had whole human eyes that had not decayed with the rest of their bodies. Each pair of eyes looked up to me. The skeletal mouths pleaded with me to help them, to release them from their purgatory. One woman seemed familiar to me. I tried to stop and help her up.

Anubis grabbed my hand pulling me along. "You can do nothing for these people. They were criminals in life and will be treated as the scum of the earth in death."

"What if they were wrongly accused? What if they are innocent?"

"Lord Osiris knows all. He would not treat innocents as criminals. Walk faster so you do not see their faces." Anubis quickened his step.

I had to hurry to keep up with him. We made it to another gate. This one was bronze. A black puppy greeted us in front of the gate. Anubis picked a small red ball out of his pocket and threw it. The puppy turned on its heels to run after the ball. As it ran after the ball, the puppy transformed into a huge black dog with three heads.

"Hurry through before he returns." Anubis slipped through the gate locking it behind us. I could feel the breath of three dog heads muss my hair as the gate locked.

We were no longer walking on skeletons. The ground was green and squishy under my feet. I didn't really want to look. I sighed. I had to know.

It was grass. We were in a meadow. The field was endless and crammed with people. It was hard to walk without bumping into someone.

"Welcome to Purgatory. This is a place for those whose bodies were not mummified and cared for when they died. There is no place in the afterlife for these types of souls. Here is where you will find Victor." Anubis bowed like he had just done me a great service.

He hadn't. Even if I could get all of these people to line up so I could search them one by one, I would be here for years. There weren't any trees for me to climb to get a higher vantage point. How was I going to find Victor in this mess? Why hadn't Adam properly seen Victor off to the other side by caring for his body?

Souls were meandering calling out the names of their loved ones. One man in a three piece suit came up to me and started shaking me. "Do you know who I am? Where am I? What is this place?"

Anubis pulled him off of me sending him back into the mess of people who wanted the same answers. "The longer you are in this place, the more you forget the things you want to remember. The more you wither away until there is nothing left of you."

"You must be looking for this, Anubis, my love."

Anubis and I tried to see who was talking but the crowd was too thick. I guess she felt the same way because she started mowing people down with her ornamental onyx dagger, the twin to the one Anubis carried. Souls cried out as they stampeded to get out of her way. Some were crushed by the surge of other souls. Some were stabbed by the dagger causing them to dissolve like they had never existed in the first place.

When life throws chaos in your direction, throw chaos back in life's face.

I grabbed the dagger from Anubis's belt and pushed my way through the throng of people. Finally we were in the center of the crowd and I could see her for who she really was. She had the head of a wolf and the body of a woman. Her mocha skin was exposed in all of the wrong places. Her sheath dress was too small and too sheer to really cover anything. Where Anubis had amber eyes, this woman had jade ones. They were two halves of the same coin. This must have been Ammut, Anubis's mate.

It was a shame I was going to have to kill her. She had her dagger to Victor's throat. If she dissolved his soul so help me God I was really going to be pissed.

"Ammut, what have you done?" Anubis took a step forward his hands up.

Like hell I was going to let him surrender to her. I stepped in front of Anubis to protect him.

"I did what I had to. I couldn't survive without you. Alexander promised me…" Ammut trailed off.

I could see she was in the same boat that Baht and I had been in. We would all put the world through unspeakable horrors to save the men we loved. Unfortunately, we never put the world through those horrors, only the other people we loved and cared about. It was a wonder any of us had any one person who still loved us at all.

Ammut dropped her hold on Victor. Anubis slipped the dagger out of my hand. I ran to Victor. When I looked behind me, I couldn't tell if Ammut and Anubis were kissing or grappling. It didn't matter. My life was dictated by doing one thing at a time. This was the time to get answers from Victor.

I touched Victor's skin, floored by another memory. No sound. No color. Just pictures moving too fast to make out what was happening. The few details I remembered were so disjointed I couldn't piece them together enough to figure out what was going on. A lab coat stained with blood. A scarred hand. Lightning.

I must have been seeing parts of what Victor did to bring Adam back, only I was seeing this memory through Victor's eyes because I hadn't been there. It was like I had caught one of Victor's memories as it left his body and used it. I didn't find it a particularly helpful memory, however, I was happy to have been gifted a memory at all.

"Victor, Victor, do you know who I am?" I pulled Victor close to me holding his face in my hands trying to get him to focus. I could see a battle out of the corner of my eye. Anubis was going to have to take care of himself.

"Sel-Selene? Are you dead?" Victor looked confused. He had been here for two hundred years. I'm surprised he remembered me at all.

"Sort of. Dead enough to find you. Look that really doesn't matter right now. Victor, I need to know where the book is." I had my arm around his frail frame.

If he didn't completely remember who I was, I could at least make it look like we had been friends. I actually couldn't really remember if we had been friends or not. My hunch was that we had been so I rolled with my gut instinct.

"What book?" Victor didn't seem scared of me which was a good thing. He didn't seem all that with it either which was a not so good thing.

"The *Book of the Dead*. Victor, you used the *Book of the Dead* to bring Cassius back to life after that pack of hellhounds tore him apart. What happened after you brought Cassius to life? Where is the book?" I was shaking Victor now. Time was of the essence. Anubis was losing his battle between good and evil and I was losing a war with time and Victor's memory.

"That's right," Victor seemed excited. Maybe we had something here. "I pieced Cassius together with bits and bobs I found in the cemetery. Then, I used the book to bring his soul back from the Underworld and put it in his new body." Victor grew quiet. He was no longer excited about bringing a man back from the dead.

"What is it, Victor? What happened when you put Cassius's soul back in his body?"

"The price for using the magic required to put a soul back in a body is to trade places with that soul in the Underworld. That's why I am here. I traded my soul for Cassius's. I don't know what happened to the *Book of the Dead*. I'm sorry, Selene." Victor began to sob into his hands.

I held him close letting him cry about what he had done, about not knowing how to help me. His soul was dissolving in my arms. What was happening? He hadn't been here long enough to waste away had he? When his soul was completely gone, I looked up. Ammut had used her dagger to release Victor's soul from this plane of existence. Anubis was lying on the ground to my left. His dagger was still in his hands. I would never be able to reach it in time. If Ammut used her dagger on me here, right now, my soul would never get back to my waiting body.

"The book is in Baht's sarcophagus. Alexander has had it all along. I pried it from Victor's cold, dead fingers." Ammut was gloating. It was not becoming on her.

I had gotten up. Maybe I could keep her talking so I could get close enough to where Anubis lay and have a fighting chance at keeping my soul.

"And where is that?" I put my hands on my hips goading her.

"Eternal Life. Where else?" She rolled her eyes at me like that should have been my first guess.

Oddly enough, when she said that I felt like it should have been my first guess too though I wasn't sure why. I had no idea what 'eternal life' meant.

"Good bye, Selene. I will not be sorry to see you go." Ammut raised her dagger meaning to stab me in the chest.

I kind of wanted it. I mean, everybody I had ever met in my entire life had tried to kill me at some point this week. If I was so horrible maybe I was meant to die.

Anubis tackled Ammut dragging her to the ground with him. They struggled to detangle themselves from the other. Anubis stabbed Ammut in the place where her heart should have been just as she stabbed him in the place where I knew his heart lay. Their particles dissolved colliding into each other until I couldn't tell where one began and the other ended. They were two soul mates forever entwined as glittering particles of light gliding on the winds of hell.

I sat on the grass in the Purgatory meadow and sobbed. I knew where the book was, I just didn't know how to go home. I was going to have to live in Purgatory for eternity or until Adam finally gave up and mummified my body. Neither were an option I wanted. I dried my face with my sleeve. I wasn't going down like this. Not today. I was determined to get back home.

I got up and started marching for the bronze gate. I would have to get past a three headed hellhound to get out. I didn't have a ball. Maybe I could find something else to distract it while I made a run for the next gate. I pressed my face to the bars on the gate trying to see where the hellhound was.

A drum was beating in my head. The ground shook to the beat of the drum making my insides vibrate. I crouched on the ground near the gate holding my head. I couldn't stop screaming. It was too painful to exist. My body started floating higher and higher until it was above the gate. The three headed dog was a puppy with one head again, until he saw me in the air. He turned back into a three headed monstrosity and leapt into the air. His middle head nipped at the heel of my shoe. I closed my eyes decidedly ready for whatever was next for me.

When I opened them I was back on my kitchen table. Adam was standing over me holding defibrillator paddles. James was on my other side ready to squeeze a syringe of something into my arm. I tried to sit up. Strong, scarred hands stopped me.

"Just rest, Selene. You're back."

I couldn't focus with the lights in my eyes. I closed my eyes then opened them staring into the light above our dining room table until salt from my tears forced them closed again. I was just in the Underworld. I had talked to Victor. I had lost Anubis.

I bolted upright. "Anubis!" I looked around the room spotting Anubis's body in a crumpled heap on the border between our living room and kitchen.

He hadn't come back with me. He hadn't made it back over the border between the living and dead. I had watched his corporal form dissolve while we were in Purgatory. I hoped for him that meant peace. I hoped for him that meant all of the shimmery particles that made him up had floated to a better place. I hoped for him this death meant he could finally be with the woman he loved not the sad, angry version of her that killed him in this life.

Chapter 13

I was epically boned in every way possible. After James took Anubis's body to Asylum's morgue to prepare him for burial, I had gone into the bathroom and cried. I started my sob-fest on the closed toilet lid with my head in my arms on the bathroom counter. That didn't last long before I ended up on the rug in front of the bathtub holding a towel around me like a security blanket. Now, I was vomiting my brains out in the sink and feeling bad about whoever had to clean that up because it certainly was not going to be me.

I rinsed my mouth with mouthwash and brushed my teeth gagging on the minty taste of both the entire time. And thinking. Gagging and thinking. Neither was good for me. I needed to find Baht's sarcophagus and maybe the *Book of the Dead* before Alexander moved it again. The only trouble was I had no idea how to get to

108

eternal life. I didn't want to have to die again to get to someplace I needed to be.

Maybe that was it. To get to eternal life you had to die. Eternal Life was the name of a church with a cemetery attached in a town about thirty minutes south of here. It couldn't be that easy, could it? If it was, I should probably take a security team and a truck with me. This was something that shouldn't wait for dawn to break. We would have to go now. While I was there, I would have to figure out what my connection to that place was. The feeling of a memory had washed over me when Ammut told me where Baht's sarcophagus was. I couldn't get the memory to recall though. I still couldn't now that I was back on this side of death. Maybe being at the cemetery would help.

Adam was standing outside of the bathroom with a cup of hot tea. "Don't go in there. Also, get your mummy raiding shoes on. We're going to steal a sarcophagus."

"There are no such things as mummy raiding shoes. And we aren't raiding anything." Adam called after me. I waved behind me as I walked out the front door of our apartment.

James was not in his office. I tried his cell phone. I could hear it ringing. I moved some papers around on his desk. And Bob's your uncle. Here was his cell phone right here. I wasn't going to find him that way. Ugh, I hated having to look for him. He needed to be chipped with a GPS so I could find him when he was clearly avoiding me.

"He's in the morgue with Anubis, Miss."

I jumped thirty feet in the air. Reginald.

"Thanks, Reggie. I'll catch up with him there." I gave Reginald a short salute and headed to the one place I really didn't want to go to find James. The morgue.

As far as morgues go, the one at Asylum was pretty state of the art. All of the equipment and tables were stainless steel. They were always spotless which was probably because we rarely needed to use them. Hell, we used the freezer drawers more. That's normally where we put our dead because at least one person was with them and knew how they died. I shuddered. I'm glad when I woke up in the morgue last week I hadn't woken up trapped in a cold, metal box alone and scared of what might be lurking in the dark with me. Although, given what I did wake up to, maybe a cold, metal box would have been better.

I stood outside of the morgue for a few minutes breathing heavily. Adam came up behind me and put his arm around my waist. I wasn't sure if I was having a panic attack because of what I had gone through at the last morgue I visited or if it was because Anubis was in there. Even though I didn't fully remember him, in the week that I had known him he had been a good friend. I didn't need him to die for me to prove that.

I closed my eyes. It was like every other time I was alone with my thoughts in the dark. Every time I close my eyes, I see the faces of the dead. The faces of the people I should have saved. The faces of the demons and monsters I killed to fuel my bad habits before I found out who I was meant to be. The faces of those I knew I shouldn't want to save, those that died at my hand because the rest of the world and some small part of myself deemed them unworthy of being saved.

The faces of the dead linger on your soul more when you're the reason why they are dead. Anubis's face will haunt my days and nights. If I could sleep his face would be the stuff of my nightmares. He will eventually chase what's left of my soul for eternity along with the others I let down in life like a pack of rabid wolves after an injured fawn. I would see that meadow in Purgatory again. I knew when I did it would never let me forget. Not like it did for the others.

I pushed my way through the swinging double doors to the morgue's office with Adam hot on my heels. James wasn't in there. I pushed through another set of doors to the morgue proper.

James was in there talking softly to Anubis's corpse and stroking his face. "I'm sorry, old friend. I should not have punished you for so long. Your betrayal was not your own."

I had just noticed Anubis had his human head back. He had worn the head of a wolf while we were in the Underworld. I guess he hadn't changed forms here, just in the Afterlife. I don't know why that bothered me but it did.

I hated to interrupt James at a moment when he was actually acting like a real person and not some gym coach from hell. "James, I need a strike team. Can you authorize that for me?"

James spun on his heels. He had his pissed off face on. Super. "Why would I authorize a strike team for you? Haven't you done enough today?"

"Ammut told me where Baht's sarcophagus was and that the *Book of the Dead* was hidden in her mummy or with her mummy or whatever. I wasn't particularly hanging on every word she said." I was coping an attitude and waving my hands in the air. I would not stand for James to be the only one in the room who acted like he had lost someone today. Also, I hated it when he bossed me around even if he was, in fact, my boss.

"Reginald," James called out to thin air.

"Yes, sir." Reginald appeared out of the same thin air James had just been shouting into.

Just like every time I see him, when Reginald showed up I jumped thirty feet in the air and clutched my chest like Dr. Morton on what he considered to be a good night.

"Selene needs a strike team ASAP. Be sure she gets everything she needs." James dismissed us with a delicate wave of his hand.

When I got to the first set of double doors, I looked behind me at James. He was stroking Anubis's hair again. It seemed odd that they had known each other and not said anything. When you have a second soul in your body dictating your every move you can't exactly trust what your eyes tell you they are seeing. Maybe James hadn't known Anubis at all and I was reading too much into a situation I knew nothing about.

Adam and I followed Reginald to the Ops room. The strike team was waiting for us.

"Selene." Gary, the team lead on duty, nodded to me.

"Gary." I nodded back.

Adam, who had served in the military in some fashion or another for majority of his life, took over. "Listen up. We are going to raid what remains of the Church of Eternal Life. Our primary objective is to secure a sarcophagus we believe is in the church's basement. The church and grounds may be littered with unfriendlies so be on your guard at all times. Gear up. We move out in five."

A couple of dozen men in military fatigues began a synchronized dance they had practiced together for years. Two men were at a supply cabinet rapidly throwing various guns, sheathed knives, grenades and other weapons into the air. Someone was always around to catch what was being thrown and put that thing in a duffle bag. Someone else would throw the bags into a pile when they were packed the way he wanted them. Someone else was handing the bags off to whoever was standing around and telling them what truck to put them in. These men were a well-oiled machine that did not need my help. I leaned against a far wall out of their way waiting for one of them to tell me what truck to get in.

Adam came over to me carrying a weapons holster with knives strung along it. I opened my mouth to ask why he hadn't brought me a gun.

"No guns. You aren't properly trained. Besides, you were always better with knives anyway." He attached the knife holster to my thigh and kissed me.

When I remembered to breathe again, I tracked him with my eyes as he went around the room checking the team's progress and gearing up himself.

"Selene, you will be in the Bravo vehicle in the back between Garrison and Marks. You are not to leave their side. Do exactly as they tell you."

I wanted to argue that I was a goddess and not a child. Gary didn't look like he was having any part of that conversation, so I nodded. Also, I wasn't entirely sure Baht's sarcophagus would even be at this church. It was just my best guess based on what Ammut told me. Let the guys do all the hard work crating her sarcophagus around and I would search for the book.

Chapter 14

Our caravan drove out of town for about twenty minutes before following the railroad tracks to the center of the little town that was our destination. The only things I saw the whole ride there were houses breaking up the muted landscape. And cows. A lot of fucking cows. Oh, yeah, they had a gas station and a post office. In the same squat white building. At the "center" of town. The caravan turned left here and kept driving for another ten minutes before off-roading onto a dirt road that we followed for I don't even know how many miles.

My life lately had been too full of color and sound. The dreary landscape of the country was somehow peaceful to me. The closer we got to the defunct church and accompanying graveyard, the more I felt like something wasn't quite right about this whole thing. When we got to Eternal Life Church, I felt off like I had just forgotten how to do anything. Walking and talking became a chore. I let Frick and Frack lead me to the church steps. I shook my head. I had a hard time thinking clearly in this place. It felt like the grounds wanted to tell me something but we didn't speak the same language.

Half of the church had burned away in a fire some years ago. No one had rebuilt the church's sanctuary leaving it open to nature and the elements. The front door was only standing because of the stonework holding up the door frame. The actual door was wood. What wasn't burned off in the fire was rotting off the hinges. Gary nodded to a guy in the front of the strike team line. That guy kicked down the door blowing it halfway into the outer sanctuary. He hadn't even kicked it that hard.

I walked in to the outer sanctuary and looked up. The moon was a sliver high in the night sky. There were no clouds. The sky was clear enough that I could see several constellations of stars that I recognized, none of which I could name. I took a deep breath of the crisp autumn air. It almost felt like this was going to be the last breath I was going to take so I needed to make the best of it.

The strike team continued on to the inner sanctuary. I was held at the door while the guys made sure it was safe. Adam nodded to Marks who led me to the back of the sanctuary. We held at the door to the stairs that led to the crypts below the church while some guys cleared the rest of the church.

"Clear." I heard someone say through Garrison's ear piece.

Despite getting the all clear, I had that prickly hairs on your neck feeling you get when you know someone is watching you. I looked behind me. I didn't see anyone. I wondered if anyone else felt like we were walking into a trap or if I should warn them. The guy at the front used a pair of bolt cutters to cut the lock on the iron bars protecting the crypt from bandits. The iron bars had the same Egyptian symbols as the ones I saw design the gates in the Underworld. Maybe these bars weren't for keeping things out. Maybe these bars were made to keep something in.

We descended a set of stone steps. One of the strike team had been tasked with keeping pace ahead of the rest of us so he could light torches all the way down. I slipped on a step slick with moisture. Garrison caught me from behind and righted me.

"Thanks," I whispered. Even my muted whisper sounded like I was shouting in the close quarters we found ourselves in.

He nodded. Military men are men of few words when on the job. That was all of the acknowledgement I was going to get.

We stopped at a landing. I didn't know how far underground we were. I could see my breath in the dim light from the torches. The guy who had been lighting the torches all the way down knelt in front of a pool. He frowned, dipped a couple of his fingers in the dark puddle and smelled them. He seemed satisfied by what he was smelling. He lit a match and dropped it into the puddle.

The entire landing lit up. The puddle must have been some kind of oil or other accelerant. We weren't on a landing at all. We were in an antechamber. We had found a tomb. Three of the walls glittered blinding me. They were gilded and all of that gold reflected the fire we had just started back at us. Hieroglyphs were carved into the gold walls. I didn't know how to read them. The fourth wall was stone with murals depicting the life of the person buried here. I didn't recognize any of the people from the pictures. In front of that stone wall were two sphinges on either side of a stone door etched with a cartouche. I ran my hand over the name written in gold hieroglyphs there. I recognized it. This was where my eternal life began. That's why it felt so familiar when Ammut mentioned it in the Underworld.

"Everyone get out now. This is my tomb not Baht's. It's a trap. Move! Move!" Men were scrambling as I was shouting orders.

I felt something large move behind me. I turned around to see the sphinges were no longer lying down. They were stretching their lion bodies and licking their paws with their human tongues. They looked bored but I wasn't taking any chances. Fully spread out they took up most of the antechamber. The entryway we had come in slid shut. We would not be able to go back that way.

The sphinx to my left stopped stretching. "Selene, we have been expecting you. You may enter." The sphinges bowed. The stone door behind them slid open.

"She doesn't go anywhere without me." Adam pulled me behind him.

"You may not enter." The second sphinx regarded Adam with a special kind of disdain teenagers reserved for the rest of the world.

Adam drew a sword out of thin air. I had no idea he had even brought one with him. Boys and their toys, sheesh. The two sphinges shrank to large man size and stood on their back legs. They still had

116

lion bodies and human heads. I thought their lion bodies would make it harder for them to fight. They drew weapons from belts I didn't know they were wearing, wielding them deftly. I guess their lion bodies weren't a detriment after all. The strike team members still left on this side of the outer door when it closed didn't amount to much. They weren't going to let this go without putting their two cents in. All of them drew some type of weapon. I stood behind Adam not wanting anyone else to die for me.

"Stop! As your queen I command you to stop." I stepped in front of Adam to address the sphinges.

"This tomb may have been built for you but you are not our queen." The sphinx to my left took a running start.

He would have ran me clean through with his blade if Adam hadn't pushed me aside to cross blades with the creature. The other sphinx was in a heated battle with the boys from the strike team. Gun fire erupted sounding like pellets of ice hitting a window. Offhand, I heard someone yell something about needing a bigger caliber of bullet.

If I didn't focus on what was in front of me I was likely to die again. I really didn't need to die again. Not right now. I couldn't get between Adam and the sphinx he was fighting. It was probably for the best. My fighting skills weren't as good as his were. Glitter caught the corner of my eye turning my head. The lighting system we had activated when we came in extended to this room too.

Beyond the only open door were treasures I never could have imagined. I meandered into the next room on my guard in case something else was feeling attacky today. The stone door slid shut behind me with a thud. I didn't try to leave. I knew my destiny was here, in this tomb. I only hoped the tomb built for me wasn't where I would last lay my head as a living soul.

I looked around the room I had purposefully trapped myself in. There were chests stacked against one of the walls. I opened the first chest I didn't have to pry open with a crowbar. It had gold coins with different hieroglyphs and faces on them. One of the coins had my mother's face on one side and a man's face on the other. The man closely resembled James though he wasn't an exact match. I pocketed the coin to study later.

Another chest had precious stones and gems. Another chest had only jewelry. I was about to close the heavy lid of the jewelry trunk when a bracelet caught my attention. I picked it up. It was identical to the bracelet I had given Adam during our last few minutes together before my first death. It had the same scarab with rubies, diamonds, emeralds and opals covering the entirety of the bracelet. The only smooth surfaces were underneath where the bracelet caressed one's skin.

I ran my hands over an engraving on the bracelet's underside. My ancient Egyptian was terrible. I recognized a family symbol that had also been etched on the cartouche on the other side of the last door I had just walked through. This had to be the same bracelet as the one I had given to Adam. Why had he not kept it safe all this time like he was supposed to? Maybe it was me, or, more specifically, Baht pretending to be me, that had moved it here. I had no memory of doing this. Then again, I didn't remember much lately.

The only vision I had seen where I mentioned the bracelet was the one where Adam and I were married. If I remembered correctly, I had told Adam that my mother was planning something and this bracelet was the key. I hadn't told him what my mother had been planning. I didn't have any Earth shattering revelations standing here in my tomb about what she had been planning either. Thing is, I stole this bracelet two millennia ago. If I was trying to stop Cleopatra from doing something, I either succeeded or I failed and there was nothing I could do about it now.

I put the bracelet on at a loss for what to do next. My plan to see what was in my tomb (since it clearly did not house my mummified corpse) was not going as I expected. Although, what did I expect really? I had never visited my own tomb before.

I sat down on one of the thrones just hanging out in the middle of the room with the other random furniture. I pulled a fur of some kind around me and started to cry. I don't know why I was so emotional. I didn't even really remember my mother. I had the sudden urge to miss her. Maybe if she hadn't killed herself she would be here with me now. She would be standing beside me holding my hand and facing my past with me. Instead of being my past she would be my future. From everything I remembered about her and had been told about her, she wouldn't be standing here trying to hold my hand or help me. She would be here reminding me about what a terrible daughter I was and possibly even be trying to kill me. I cried harder. I just wanted her to love me. It had been two millennia since I had spent my days vying for her love and approval. Why did I crave it so much now?

The smell of rotting food found the inside of my nostrils. It was customary to bury royalty after mummification in a tomb with everything they would need in the afterlife including food. I held my stomach retching over the side of the throne I had taken residence. I wiped my mouth on the fur covering my back as I stumbled to the corner where all of the food had been placed. I picked up a jug uncorking it. Good. It was wine. No telling how long it had been down here. Hopefully, the age will make it taste decent. I took a swig rinsing out my mouth. I spit the dirty wine on the sand and limestone beneath my feet. Someone else could clean that up.

I carried the wine jug by the handle through the doorway to the next antechamber of my tomb. Let's see what else Alexander thought I would need in the afterlife. This wasn't a chamber at all. It was a hallway. There was light here as well. Whatever grief I was legally required by law as his sister to give him would be overshadowed by the praise I had at Alexander's ingenuity in building this tomb. I didn't see any oil puddles. How he got each room to feed off of the other and light the whole tomb with one match was kind of astounding.

A rat scurried over my foot. I jumped back dropping the jug of wine. I'll admit, I kind of screamed. Only a little. And since no one was there to witness my scream let's just say it was a delicate, lady-like scream. Yeah, let's go with that.

I looked down. The wine was travelling in a pattern on the floor. It looked like a great serpent guiding my way. I stepped to the left side of the snake wanting to follow it down the hall. When I did, the stone I stepped on sank into the floor. An arrow whizzed out of the

119

wall to my right. I ducked narrowly avoiding being impaled. I guess it wouldn't have mattered if I died here. It was my tomb after all.

Still crouched on the floor, I looked around. Just like my asshole brother to booby trap my eternal resting spot so I couldn't break in without dying first. I noticed the serpent was weaving its way on top of certain stones. It was a longshot. I decided to follow the inadvertent wine trail I had left myself. I took a chance and stood up fully. For me, fully was only five feet. Let's hope none of those arrows were angled down during construction. I put one foot on the tail of the serpent and ducked. Nothing happened. I waited a second just to be sure Alexander's booby traps weren't on a time delay or something. Nothing. Good. I straightened back up being careful to only step on the stones the wine snake touched.

On the other side I turned back. The hallway hadn't been as long as it appeared from where I started. I touched the toe of my sneaker to the nearest stone not covered in wine and jumped back. Good thing I did because a column of fire shot up from underneath the stone I had just depressed. Satisfied I would never leave my tomb alive, I kept moving.

Chapter 15

The door was locked. This was the first door I had come across that wasn't already open or didn't open when I drew near. Maybe they were like the automatic doors at supermarkets. I jumped back and forth in front of it. To be fair, when I tried to get into places with automatic doors they never opened for me, so I was already certain that wasn't going to work. I knocked on the door. No answer. I screamed a few obscenities. Nothing. I sat down with my back to the door.

I needed a break. Not just from this little adventure but from my entire life. Deep down I could feel the years I had lived closing in on me. It would be so easy to give in, to stay down here forever, to let Baht take her place in my body, to let someone else become me so I didn't have to live for one more day like this. There comes a point in your life when you stop living and you merely exist, when you wonder why you're still living, still trying, why you're still here and if you even want to be anymore.

I wasn't all too sure I wanted to continue living. Especially if it meant living with Baht grappling for control of my body. I could feel her now trying to escape the prison Madame Cosmescu built for her. What was the point in continuing this existence if it meant the child I knew I was carrying could be Alexander's and not Adam's? Especially if it meant I was birthing evil incarnate. Again. I couldn't kill another child no matter how much wrong they'd done.

I considered jumping off the ledge of my current safe haven and trying to hit as many stones as I could when I landed. I didn't know what kind of traps I would set-off if I carried out my plan. I did know these traps could, and probably would, kill me. I will admit I stood there for a long time. I couldn't move forward. The door to my past was locked and I didn't have a key. The way back to my future was easy if I could just get my foot off the precipice, if I just had the balls to do something I had never done before. I had my foot lifted over the edge. I could do it.

"Selene, stop!"

I looked up. Adam was standing at the other side of the hallway. I wasn't sure if he wanted me to stop because he knew what I was about to do or if he just wanted me to wait for him. He took another step towards the floor of death. A handful of strike team guys were behind him filing into the room.

"Adam, wait. The floor is booby trapped." I shouted to him.

I know he heard me because he stopped walking and pushed the strike team back. I was happy to see Garrison and Marks were still alive. I didn't want to hear about the other guys. I hoped they were alive too and just resting at the entrance. My heart knew better.

"How did you get across?" Adam shouted.

"Only step on the stones the serpent touches," I called back.

It was actually kind of comical to watch a group of huge football player sized men walk in a straight line, heel to toe, with their arms stretched holding the shoulders of the man in front of them. They looked like elephants on a tightrope during a circus. One by one they crossed to the safe zone. No one got impaled or burned. This day was starting to look up. For all of us, I guess.

From what I could see of the motley crew that came to my aid, they were all injured in some way. Adam had a few makeshift stitches above his right eye. His shirt was covered in sand and blood. I would have to ask him later if the sphinges had bleed when he killed them or just turned back to sand.

"You were standing here because you have no idea how to open this door weren't you?" Adam gave me his patented, trademark pending, glare.

"No," my voice trailed off. I wasn't about to tell him when I quit trying to figure out how to get past the door, I had been contemplating suicide.

Adam ran his hands over the door before giving his official assessment. "We need a key."

I threw my hands up in the air. "Of course we need a key because that is the one thing I actually brought with me tonight."

Adam grabbed my wrist sharply. The look on my face said unhand me. The look on his face said he hadn't meant to grab me that hard.

"The carving above the keyhole looks like a scarab. Where did you pick this up?" Adam turned my wrist over investigating the bracelet.

"Do you remember when I gave this to you? Do you remember our wedding night when I told you my mom was planning something and this was the key?" I took the bracelet off to wave in his face.

"I do." Adam's face was solemn.

"What did I tell you? What was my mother planning?" My voice started loud trailing off until the sounds I was making grew quieter. I rambled on until I was speaking just above a whisper. "Did I stop her?"

"I don't know what she was planning back then. You never told me. I guess whatever you did stopped her." Adam took my hands in his.

"What did you do with this bracelet when I gave it to you? Where did you hide it? How did it get here?" My voice was getting shrill. My stomach was churning. I was going to throw up again.

Adam looked down. He knew he was in trouble. "Just before I was attacked by that pack of hellhounds, I grew weary of carrying the weight of the world around in such a small package. I gave the bracelet to Shifu. He is a dragon. I knew he would keep it safe since dragons hoard and guard gold and precious metals. I don't know how it got here. I haven't seen Shifu once these past two hundred years." Adam looked up. He was thinking about the fate of his old friend. I could see the pain in his eyes. We had both lost so much for a cause that meant so little to us.

I tossed the bracelet to him. The time for empty words and meaningless apologies to each other was over. The time to act was now.

Adam fumbled the bracelet dropping it on the stone floor. The scarab cracked in half revealing a piece of parchment and a small key with an ornamental scarab adorning the key's bow. It looked identical to the key Reggie carried in his pocket to use on secret doors at Asylum. Adam handed me the parchment and put the pieces of bracelet in his backpack.

I unfurled the scroll. "Adam, I can't read this." I handed him the parchment and turned my head to wipe my eyes. I was emotional again but I was determined not to cry in front of what was left of my strike team.

"It looks like a legend of some kind." Adam handed the parchment back.

I folded it up and put it in the back pocket of my jeans. I had been right all those years ago. The bracelet was a key. Well, the bracelet contained a key. For what, I wasn't sure. I thought the bracelet would change the world. I guess I was right. The bracelet was changing my world at least by opening this door for me. Adam turned the small scarab key in the lock. The door cracked in half becoming a set of double doors that swung into the next room. At last, we were entering the burial chamber where Baht's sarcophagus lay.

The room was simply adorned with no furniture, only a large wooden chapel inscribed with coffin texts and a small funeral chest. The walls were covered in paintings of the process of mummification and travel to the afterlife. I touched one of Anubis in his wolf form guiding a soul to the Underworld. I would miss him until my own dying day. I hoped Osiris found him so he could reprise his role of guiding souls to their eternal rest. I hoped one day I would see him again when my body finally died and my soul would be allowed to exist in the Afterlife. It didn't matter if my soul got to rest in the Afterlife. I just wanted to be able to exist there, to be able to see my friend again, to apologize to Sylvia and all of the other people who had died because of my actions without knowing why.

"Anyone bring a crowbar?" Adam was testing the locks on the chapel and chest.

"Try this," Gary handed Adam a hand-held battering ram.

Adam used the flat end to break off the locks on the chest and the chapel. I opened the chest first finding what I expected- Baht's internal organs mummified in their own canopic jars. There were four total. If the priest who mummified Baht did it correctly, the jar with the sculpture of the human head held her liver, the jackal head jar held her stomach, the ape head jar held her lungs and the falcon head jar held her intestines. I wasn't going to open every jar to find out if she was mummified properly or not. I didn't care that much.

I pushed the chest aside and stood by the chapel. There were technically four chapels, or sarcophagus boxes, around Baht's sarcophagus. I don't know why Egyptians did this. I guess I was absent the day my royal tutor taught us about the afterlife. Once all four boxes were opened, Adam was able to slide Baht's sarcophagus into the open room.

"I still can't believe you made it past the traps I left. Well done." I didn't have to turn around to know that was Alexander clapping like a jackass behind us.

Everyone else turned around anyway so I followed suit. "Alex, hey, what's up? Long time no see."

Alexander rolled his eyes. He still had the air of royalty about him even though our family hadn't ruled in millennia.

He looked weird like he was hollow. I stepped around some of the strike team guys to get a better sense of what was wrong with Alexander besides his personality.

"Selene, don't go near him. You know what he's capable of." Adam grabbed by upper arm close to my shoulder.

I wrenched free, "I know full well what he's capable of," and marched over to Alexander.

Just as I suspected, it wasn't Alexander at all just some cheap magic trick. I ran my hands back and forth through Alexander's torso. My hands went right through him.

Alexander laughed. "It's a hologram, Selene."

"I was hoping you were a ghost. At least then I could exorcise you and get rid of you forever." I moved back by Adam folding my arms across my chest.

"I still can't believe you made it past the traps I left. Well done." Alexander rolled his eyes.

"You just said that." I looked at Adam who shrugged his shoulders.

Alexander laughed. "It's a hologram, Selene."

"What the hell? Someone find the off switch for that stupid recording." I was yelling now. I guess the guys had heard about my temper because they scattered to try and figure out how Alexander was projecting a pre-recorded hologram. What I wanted to know was if his pre-recorded hologram came with more than two sentences. "When you find the device bring it with us in a way that it will still work. I want to know what's on it."

Adam and I held hands as we stared down Baht's sarcophagus. Her sarcophagus was the only beautiful thing about her. The person depicted on the lid of the sarcophagus had a gold face and gold hands. The eyes were lined underneath with kohl. The headdress was made of turquoise and lapis. An emerald and onyx cobra poised to strike formed the diadem laid over the headdress. The arms were crossed over the chest while the hands held an ankh and a jeweled staff. The arms each had several bracelets made out of precious stones. Bitch really knew how to do death right.

"We should open it and make sure both Baht and the book are in there." Just looking at Adam, I knew he was thinking the same thing. Neither of us actually wanted to open her sarcophagus though.

Adam signaled a few of the unoccupied, more able-bodied members of the strike team to help him push open the lid of Baht's sarcophagus.

"Here goes nothing," He deadpanned as he cracked the seal on Baht's last known resting place.

We noticed the smell before we saw the state of her corpse. There was nowhere for me to vomit so I retched on the ground next to her sarcophagus. Adam held my hair and rubbed my back. I'm sure he suspected what I already knew. He didn't comment though. One thing at a time.

When I was done emptying my stomach, Adam lifted the lid the rest of the way. Even for a mummy, Baht was sure looking rough. Her mummy mask was decaying which was odd because gold never tarnishes. I saw the Eye of Horus around Baht's neck before I realized the eye was carved all along the inside of the sarcophagus. The Eye of Horus was said to protect against and combat evil. I wondered if Baht's mummy mask was decaying when it shouldn't have because all of her evil was trapped here in a tiny box unable to escape because of the eye. Did I just unleash all of that evil on the world by opening this box? God, I hope not. That was not something I wanted to deal with today.

What was left of Baht's mummy was holding something wrapped in gilded fabric. I took it out of her hands. Pulling back the fabric I could see more hieroglyphs. This must be the *Book of the Dead.*

"Close her back up. Let's get out of here." I covered the book and put it in Adam's backpack.

Adam and Gary created a wheeled cart from some parts they had in their bags. They tied ropes on the cart and sarcophagus to keep them together and have a way to pull the two ton casket behind us.

"What are you guys doing?" I had my hands on my hips expecting Gary and Adam to make more sense than they did now. "Just tarp the remains and haul her out of here. We don't need the whole sarcophagus."

Gary and Adam looked at each other. If the look they gave each other could talk it would say "no, you tell her."

"What aren't you telling me?" I was not thrilled by what I knew was coming next.

Gary found what could only be described as pluck. "James said if we found Baht's sarcophagus to bring it home intact or not to come back at all."

I hated that people were more afraid of James than me. I also didn't think we needed to waste our time lugging around a two ton coffin, but if I could take it back to Asylum and shove it up James's ass, I would. There was something about that guy that I hated.

"We couldn't find the holograph mechanism." Marks ran up to stand between me and Gary. I could have sworn he did it on purpose.

"Leave it. Grab your gear. We're moving out." Adam was taking charge again and it was hot.

Damn hormones. I didn't have time to spend the rest of my life vomiting or jumping my husband every time he talked. This was going to be a long pregnancy.

We made it all the way to the next room when we realized we couldn't get the sarcophagus past the booby traps.

"What if we all cross without setting anything off then pull the sarcophagus along on a length of rope. It should be protected from arrows and it's made of stone so fire shouldn't damage it. I mean, Baht's already dead so what have we got to lose?" I was biting my fingernails and pacing the safe zone by the doorway.

Adam and Gary looked at each other and shrugged.

"You heard the lady, move out." Gary directed the men to go in front of and behind me while leaving a few paces between us in case anyone accidently stepped off the serpent path.

Gary led the men across. Adam picked up the rear uncoiling a rope behind him. When Adam was safely across, the men each grabbed a part of the rope and pulled. The weight of the sarcophagus set off every trap Alexander had left for us, for me. I was right though- the arrows bounced off and the fire did nothing except leave a black streak on the lid.

One thing I had not accounted for was that the floor would drop out from under the sarcophagus. That was one trap I had not encountered during my tests earlier. Unluckily for us, the floor dropped out from under the middle of the sarcophagus meaning we had to find a way to lift the back end over the hole and continue pulling it through the rest of the tomb.

"What do we do now?" I looked to Adam who was clearly thinking very hard about this problem. I could tell by the way his face made him look constipated.

"We wait." Adam sat down with his back to the wall.

I sat next to him and laid my head on his lap. "Wait for what?"

"Me."

I sat up. James was here, in my tomb, in a three piece suit looking like the devil inhabited the body of a fashion designer.

"How?" I started to ask how James knew we needed him here. He cut me off.

"Some of the men got out before the sphinx closed the tomb door. They called for back-up. Judging by the carnage in the other room, you could have used a larger strike team." James paced the safe zone staring at our heavy sarcophagus problem from every angle he could.

A handful of guys who worked for Asylum came into the chamber with long boards and ropes. The got to work using a grappling hook to string a rope from the chamber ceiling so a guy could dangle from it above the sarcophagus without touching the floor. He used his new position to tie a rope around the back end of the sarcophagus. The men with boards stood by at the ready. The guy on the ceiling drilled a hole and inserted a pulley hook. He fed the rope that he had tied to the sarcophagus through one end of the pulley. When it was long enough, he threw the free end to some guys standing in our safe zone.

Gary came to the edge of the safe zone to supervise. "Pull on my mark." He addressed the man on the ceiling and the men on the ground, "Now."

Everyone started pulling. The back end of the sarcophagus lifted a few inches off the floor. Men were holding that rope in place while some other guys pulled the rope connected to the front of the sarcophagus. With the back end lifted, they were able to bring the sarcophagus forward.

A flame burst from the ceiling narrowly avoiding the guy harnessed there. Instead, it hit the rope holding the back end of the sarcophagus causing the sarcophagus to come crashing down with a resounding thud. Every single person in that chamber held their breath waiting for another booby trap to go off. None did.

When we all exhaled, Gary asked the guy in suspended animation, "How are we looking on your end, Carothers?"

"One good pull ought to do it, sir. We're barely off the edge." Carothers wiped the sweat from his brow with his sleeve. He had clearly been thinking what we were thinking. Lady Luck must have been watching over him tonight.

"Alright, boys, on my mark." Gary followed suit and wiped his face with his sleeve too. "Now."

Anyone who was touching a rope was pulling. They got the sarcophagus to the end of the booby traps with only a few more arrows flying. All they needed to do now was fashion another pulley system to get the sarcophagus over the edge of the walkway to the safe zone. There was a four inch step up they had to navigate with the pulley system. Carothers wasn't waiting for an order. He lowered himself down his rope and kicked off the wall to swing over to the safe zone. Marks and some other guy caught Carothers pulling him down to safety.

Some guy who probably didn't volunteer for the job was crawling up the wall to the ceiling like a spider. He installed another pulley system in an area closer to the safe zone. He fed one end of the rope through the pulley system. The other end of the rope was tied to the front end of the sarcophagus and threw it back to whoever wanted it on the ground.

"Now." Gary started the men on pulling the riggings all over again.

They were able to wrench the sarcophagus to the safe zone until they got to a back wheel. It had gotten stuck again. The guy on the ceiling sighed and hung his head. He lowered himself down to the sarcophagus catching a rope someone threw to him on the way down. He tied one end of that rope to the back of the sarcophagus then climbed his way back to the ceiling. He held the rope in his teeth while he unspooled the rope they used to pull the front end of the sarcophagus. Once he was done, he threw that rope to Carothers and spooled the rope for the back end through the pulley. He gave Gary a thumbs up signal when he was done.

"Last time, ladies. Now." Gary swirled his index finger in the air.

Men hauled both ropes until the sarcophagus was fully in the safe zone. They guy on the ceiling rappelled down in the same way Carothers had.

"Move her out to the truck." Gary stepped away from the door letting the strike team guys figure out the best way to get Baht's mummy to the truck.

Adam and I followed with Gary and James. When we got into the treasure chamber, I saw a forensic team packing everything into crates. I felt for the coin with my mother's face on it in my pocket. It was still there.

"I have decided that since this tomb was meant for you and you are still alive despite your attempts at the contrary, we should bring everything back to Asylum to ascertain any clues as to Alexander's whereabouts or plan." James was matter of fact in an over-important way.

I didn't care what he or Asylum did with any of this stuff. This tomb may have been meant for me, none of it would actually ever be mine. I had the *Book of the Dead*. I had a picture of my mother even though it was on a coin. I had the bracelet I gave Adam before I killed myself the first time. I had everything I needed from this place.

We walked through the last chamber. The battle with the sphinges had been bloody and unnecessary. I couldn't look at the carnage, the blood on the sand, the open eyed stares of the men from the strike team who had died for me, the face of the sphinx who I knew was my enemy, who I felt sorry for anyway.

I was nauseous again. Adam walked beside me shielding my eyes from the worst parts of the battle. Following the sarcophagus through the tomb, up the stairs and out of the sanctuary was slow and tedious. I knew the sarcophagus wasn't light by any means, but I was having a hard time being in this place anymore. I wanted to jump on top of the sarcophagus, run across it and just keep running until I ran out of road or until my legs fell off.

So many things were my fault that I never intended. The deaths of those men was only one thing on a list of so much that could have been prevented had I died and stayed dead when my mom decided we should commit suicide together. This wasn't the only time that I wished I had stayed dead the first time I died. Unless something changed drastically in my lifetime, I would spend an eternity wishing I was dead, never being able to stay that way.

I was grateful the drive back would take a while. I needed to think about a lot of things that I didn't want to.

Chapter 16

Back at Vampireville, we put Baht's sarcophagus in the morgue. We really didn't have a better place to store it unless we put it in a closet somewhere. I had a terrible idea that James and Adam would have no choice but to agree to. Basically, just like my last terrible idea. The only problem with this idea (yes, aside from being horrific) was that I had no idea what I was doing. Okay. Okay. You are absolutely correct in assuming I never know what I am doing. It's just that this feels worse because I had to use magic. Let me tell you, I am *no* fan of magic. It has never done anything useful for me. Normally, all magic ever did was fuck me over with its rules and exceptions.

"Okay, so you are telling me that you have Baht imprisoned in your mind and the cage Madame Cosmescu built to trap Baht won't hold for long." James was pacing the morgue trying to figure out a way to say no to my latest hair-brained scheme.

"Right so far." I paced beside him. I had too much nervous energy to stand still.

"So you need to use the *Book of the Dead* to put her soul back into her mummified corpse and trap her there forever?" James and I bumped into each other.

"Right." I untangled myself from him after our collision.

"That seems quite spiteful. Why don't you just send her soul to the Underworld and keep the natural order of things?" James was frowning.

He didn't like for me to be the one to pass judgement on a soul. That was Osiris's domain. Only, Osiris was not in the Underworld. At least, he hadn't been when Anubis and I had gone down there. Maybe he was just taking a pee break or something and he was back there now. Maybe Alexander did something to him. That was our real problem. It didn't matter what we did with Baht's soul. Alexander would always find a way to undo all of our hard work.

"Maybe I have earned the right to be spiteful. Also, if Osiris wants her so bad he can ferry her soul to the Underworld from her mummified corpse. Anubis is no longer around to do tedium things for him." I put my hands on my hips and got in James's face. I didn't care that he was my boss. I cared that this was my body and it had an unwelcome presence housed within.

Adam was silent during this exchange. He was busy reading the *Book of the Dead* and frowning.

"What now?" I was tired. I was hungry. I was pissed. This was my normal, except this time I was tired, hungry and pissed for two.

Adam had suspected what I did and made me take a pregnancy test when we got back. It was positive. Mazel tov to me and whoever the father was.

"This book does not tell us how to ferry a soul to the Underworld or move a soul from one body to another." Adam hadn't stopped frowning since the positive pregnancy test. I don't know if it was because he didn't think he was the father or if he thought the child would be evil either way.

"What does it say then?" I went to stand next to him and try to read the book.

That couldn't be possible. The *Book of the Dead* was supposed to be for things like ferrying souls to the Underworld.

"It tells us the proper rituals for burial including the mummification process. That is unencrypted. There is a piece in the back that very well may be what we need. I can't tell because that section is encrypted. Only someone like Anubis or Osiris would have the key to unlocking the hidden texts." Adam was still flipping through the book looking for a guide on how to use it.

"Makes sense," James started, "how to send someone to the afterlife should be common knowledge, while how to bring someone back from the Underworld should be something no one should know how to do. Otherwise, everyone would pull an Alexander and bring their loved ones back. Then, the Underworld would be empty and the natural balance would be disrupted."

Have I mentioned lately how much I hate magic and all of its bullshit rules?

I rolled my eyes at James while I flipped through the book I had taken from Adam. "This looks a lot like the markings on that parchment we found in the bracelet." I pulled the paper out of my back pocket glad I hadn't decided to change when I got back.

Adam took the parchment and the book from me. "I think I can do this spell. It doesn't look like we need much. Maybe just some sage to cleanse the room." Adam kept flipping pages and murmuring to himself.

"Reginald, bring enough sage to burn and have a strike team surround this room." James said all of this out loud. It always amazed me that he never had to call Reggie on his cell phone or use some type of intercom system. As a griffin, I guess Reggie was just always around protecting James in some way.

It wasn't long before a strike team invaded the room circling us and the sarcophagus. I waved at Marks and Garrison. Marks rolled his eyes. Garrison waved back. He was my favorite anyway.

"Get this sarcophagus open." James pointed to Baht's coffin.

A couple of strike team guys pulled the lid off the sarcophagus exposing Baht's mummy. They slid the sarcophagus lid on another morgue table they had rolled up next to the table the sarcophagus was on.

I shuddered. I couldn't wait to get Baht out of my body and back into her own. I got what James was saying about me passing eternal judgement by trapping her in her mummified corpse instead of sending her to the Underworld so Osiris could pass judgement. I thought hell was too good for her. I wanted her to suffer the way she made me suffer all these years.

Reginald showed up with the sage and cleansed the room.

"Selene, stand here." Adam positioned me by Baht's head and read the spell.

Two souls connected

Eternity bound

A joining of sun and moon

What was done is now undone

Nothing happened. I just stood there like an idiot listening to Baht cackle inside of my head. I was stepping forward to yell at Adam when I fell to the floor.

I couldn't move. All I could do was lay there staring at the ceiling listening to Adam's shouts of concern. I felt the same as I had during my mummification process. I was paralyzed and completely cognizant of everything that was happening around me. Baht's soul couldn't enter my body again. It was already there. So, I waited. I counted ceiling tiles. I got up to twelve when something started to happen.

I could feel my body convulsing. Was I having a seizure? Do people who have seizures know when they are having them? My mouth opened against my will. I could see a black mass leaving my body. I was crying. When that black mass left my body I felt so light and free.

The black mass was swirling above us like it didn't have anywhere else to go. Adam started reading from the book again.

In the space of time

When one shall live

The other shall die

I could hear the pain in Baht's screams as her soul was forced back into her mummified body. I actually felt a little sorry for her. I mean she was evil, sure, but she didn't ask to be brought back by her jerk of a husband. For all we know she was having a great time in hell when Alexander's selfishness started a chain of events that royally fucked her over.

All of the air was sucked out of the room like a vacuum. It came back in just as fast as it had gone out. I hadn't realized I had stopped breathing until all of the air came back into the room and some of it forced its way into my lungs.

I sat up struggling to correct my breathing. Adam came to my side and helped me up. I hung over the side of Baht's sarcophagus. I thought the eyes of her mummy moved to the side to look at me. I couldn't be sure. One eye was still covered by part of her mummy mask.

"Close it up. Put a chain around the outside and put the sarcophagus in room Alpha Seven. Make sure there is a twenty-four hour guard on that room. Priority level red." James was ordering the strike team guys around. He turned to me and Adam, "I'll take this." James took the *Book of the Dead* out of Adam's hands closing the key inside. He handed the book to Reginald. They both disappeared before I could blink.

"What do you want to do now?" I turned to Adam glad he was holding me up right now.

"Let's spend the next six months in bed." Adam picked me up and carried me away from my past once and for all.

Chapter 17

I couldn't sleep. It didn't take long for memories to filter into my consciousness. When they started, they never stopped. Now that Baht was out of my head, I was remembering the things we did together. I was remembering the people we killed. I was remembering the hurt and pain I caused. None of the memories were anything I particularly wanted to brag about. All of the memories were things I regretted even though it wasn't me who actually did them.

I tossed and turned trying to get comfortable in my new bed of lies and misery. I didn't know if what I was remembering were things Baht actually did, or if the memories were more benign and tainted by the evil from her soul. I was also sure I wasn't getting the full picture of what Baht had done as me. Some of what I was seeing in my fretful dreams were really Baht's memories left in my body like a sense memory after a trauma. There were flashes of blood and hopelessness but nothing I could pinpoint as a singular event.

I hoped that the memories of my body hurting people and reveling in their blood were just things my brain was making up to fill the voids in time and space that I needed to have filled in order to feel whole again. I hoped that my imagination was running wild and Baht hadn't left me the gift of knowledge that I had wished for at Alexander's cabin. The trauma my body and mind suffered at the hands of Baht and Alexander would never be forgotten. Whether I found out what actually happened or not, I would have my revenge. Justice would be dealt with a swift hand wielding an onyx dagger.

I woke up in the middle of the day. We had just gone to bed when the sun rose. At least that's what the bedside clock said at the time. Living underground, it was hard to know when it was day or night unless you looked at the right clock or talked to the right person.

I clutched my stomach. Something wasn't right.

Adam sat up in bed next to me. "What's wrong?" He leaned over me to turn on a bedside lamp.

The dim lighting made everything worse. The bed was soaked with blood. My blood.

I started crying, not from the pain but the frustration of it all.

Adam got out of bed hastily pulling on a pair of boxers. He ran out of the room, presumably down the hall to sound the alarm. I laid back letting all of my blood and tears leech from my body. I knew in my heart the blood was my baby dying. I doubted my baby took after me in any way. I doubted my baby would survive being tied to me in this life or the next.

It hurt more this time than when I was pregnant with Ophelia because I was mentally present for this pregnancy. Last time, Baht got to be pregnant in my body. This time, I got to be pregnant in my body and I had screwed it up somehow. This was all my fault. Even though I didn't know if the baby was Adam's or Alexander's, I still wanted to carry it to term. I still wanted to try to teach it right from wrong. I still wanted to be the one to decide if it was evil or if it had the capacity for good. Now, I won't ever get that chance.

An Asylum doctor came back with Adam. She grabbed my arm and inserted a needle. I could feel my body floating. It reminded me of one of the times I died last year before I found out who Alexander was, before I recovered any of my memories from the times Baht wasn't in my head controlling my body, before I knew my mother was still alive. When the drug the doctor gave me reached the best parts of my veins, I dreamed. Not about my future without the baby I just lost or about losing Ophelia twice, but about the time I was killed by a demon at the *Amenity Emporium*- where life is cheap and death is free.

~

"Great, another demon spotted at Amenity Emporium. That's the third one this week! What is Amenity Emporium? A portal straight to hell or something?" I muttered to myself as I put on my gear— a crossbow I was barely adequate at using, a few small knives I couldn't throw well enough to hit the broad side of a barn, and a gun with big enough bullets that I didn't really have to aim.

Why did I have to keep pushing my feelings aside so I could deal with everyone else's? Why did it fall on me to save humanity from folding in on itself? It didn't matter. Demons were afoot and I had to be the one to send them back to the spaces in between where they came from.

I was in a parking garage Asylum used to store the vehicles of its residents retrieving my gear from the trunk of my car. I remember this demon attack in particular because it happened right after I broke up with Marcus who was the Alpha of a pack of werewolves in the city. I guess I've just spent my whole life attracting the wrong kind of weirdo and forcing their hearts to break in crooked lines making them hard to put back together.

Javier, the vampire who lived across the hall from me, was out in the parking garage smoking a joint. "Chica," he started in on me as he helped me adjust the crossbow on my back.

"Javi, just don't. He asked me to marry him. I mean really. If he knew me as well as he claimed, he never would have asked in the first place let alone in front of his entire pack." I was throwing my arms around in exasperation nearly hitting Javier in the face.

Javier ducked low looking annoyed. "I get it. I really do. Werewolves have no tact. They don't wait for the time to be right they just do whatever they feel like whenever they feel like. Be careful though. You might have just made a really powerful enemy." Javier took a drag of his joint blowing the smoke away from me.

"Fine. I'll add him to the growing list. You can never have enough enemies or your life will get too boring." I got in my car.

Javier knocked on my window dragging the last bit of smoke from between his fingers. I was so absorbed in my own life I didn't notice him ninja slink behind me from the trunk to the driver door. Damn vampires and their stupid ninja skills.

"What?" I threw out impatiently.

"My lady," he giggled, "Just so you know, even if you would have married Marcus and became the Alpha female of a pack of wolves, I would have followed you anywhere. You were my friend when I first moved to town and had none and remained my friend when you found out what I really was." He bowed low no longer a giggly school girl in the body of a ripped young man.

"It's hard to hate you when you and I are the same. And knock off that bowing shit, amigo." I waved as I peeled out of the parking garage, screeching my tires without meaning to. By the time I finally made it across town, the demon was nowhere near where the Asylum dispatcher said it had been spotted last.

"Why can't demons ever just stay in one place and wait there until I have time to kill them?" I shouted banging the steering wheel with my palms.

A lady and her small children getting into a van parked next to my car looked at me. The woman wore startled well on her face. It must have been her blonde hair and blue eyes that held the circle her mouth made in such a way as to make me think she was a model.

I held my cell phone up pretending I was yelling at someone on the other end of the line so they wouldn't alert the authorities about the crazy lady screaming at herself in the middle of the Amenity Emporium parking lot. Or worse, the Amenity Emporium manager. He was a little creep named Trey with a real hard-on for watching ladies change in his dressing rooms. I had interacted with him more than I would like to talk about in creepier ways each time. I was pretty sure he was a demon. I couldn't prove it. Without that proof Asylum wouldn't let me kill him. Killjoys.

I texted dispatch to see if the demon had been spotted anywhere else. No one had reported seeing it, so I drove my car to the *back of the garden center hoping to get lucky. I managed to find the demon. He was ugly as most demons are. It's really the good-looking demons you have to watch out for. They blend in to the crowd and you can't tell the good guys from the bad. The things I see in the dark are far worse than any you could imagine in the light.*

The demon was carelessly grazing on an elderly man. I got out of my car as silently as I could, trying to get closer without either spooking the demon (because I was so not in the mood to chase him) or having him charge at me (because I was so not in the mood to die. Again).

The elderly man had on a blue Amenity Emporium vest and name tag. Apparently Fred was an Amenity Emporium greeter who must have tasted delicious because the demon wasn't leaving any left-overs. I got out my cross-bow and fired a few shots. One actually hit the mark just not in a place that would turn it to dust upon impact. Plus, I think he turned into the shot. Out of sheer stupidity probably.

Much like anyone else I have ever interacted with in my entire life, I pretty much only succeeded in pissing it off. It charged me. I fired some shots from the gun. I don't know if I hit it and didn't faze it one bit or if I missed completely. Either way, I was totally fucked because it was all over me in seconds.

Demons always smell to me like Sulphur and something else I could never place though it always made me feel like I was home. The demon stepped on my left arm and broke it in several places. I'm not going to lie. It hurt like a motherfucker and I screamed like a little girl. Power to anyone who can remain stoic as a demon is beating the shit out of them. I cannot. I have an intense aversion to pain and suffering especially when it comes to my pain and suffering. The demon bent to deliver its kiss of death at the same time as I was driving my knife into its chest. The pain burned my skin like fire kissing ice.

The demon didn't turn to dust like I had hoped. The knife stuck in its chest. It was backing away. I couldn't let it leave and hurt someone else. As the edges of my world started to dim, I felt the cool metal of my gun brush my fingertips. Instead of giving into my desire to close my eyes and sleep forever, I renewed my resolve grasping for the gun with my non-broken arm, finally reaching it. I grappled with

145

trying to pick up the shotgun with one hand for only a fraction of a second. It felt like an eternity. I won the war I was waging on gravity. Gun now in hand I braced my good arm with the bad and fired three shots hoping at least one of them made its mark. My breath grew labored as the demon dusted itself into the shifting wind getting all over me. I squinted trying not to let the dust get in my eyes. I thought I saw my mother standing above me, comforting me, letting me know it was okay to let this world go to be where she was. I felt warm and safe so I closed my eyes. "Just for a second," I reasoned.

Chapter 18

I woke up in the medical wing. I didn't hurt anymore. I couldn't feel anything at all. I lethargically stared down at the IV running from my left arm to a machine on a thin metal pole. The machine beeped sending medicine to my veins putting me to sleep again.

Chapter 19

Adam was brushing my hair with his fingers. It took more effort than it should have to open my eyes and keep them open.

"Selene?" Adam stopped running his fingers through my hair to adjust my blankets.

I felt miserable. I was cold. I was nauseous. Most importantly, I didn't care. I could have died and I would have welcomed Death like an old friend I no longer held a grudge against. I knew what happened. I had to ask anyway. "What's going on?" My voice came out as a whisper. I choked on the sterile hospital air.

Adam spooned some ice chips into my mouth. I let them melt before swallowing them. When my mouth was empty, he spooned in more. The third time he tried to feed me I pushed his hand away. Adam sat back in the spare chair by the bed looking dejected. He was just as upset as I was about the loss of our baby. I could tell he also thought it was his fault. How could it be his fault if I was the one who was carrying the baby and couldn't protect it? It. I didn't even know if it was a boy or a girl. I started sobbing.

"Selene," Adam sighed. He started by patting my hair then moved to patting my shoulder. He had never been at a loss when it came to comforting me. Why was this time any different?

It didn't matter. I didn't see how our relationship could have survived when Adam knew some of the things I did with Alexander, when he suspected, like I did, the baby I was carrying was Alexander's and not his. I pushed his hand away and rolled to my side turning my back on him. He covered me up with the blanket. I heard him sigh heavily. As he sat back down in the chair, it scooted back slightly scraping on the tile floor of my hospital room. The sound was deafening interrupting the silence my life was now shrouded in. My shoulders slowed as they heaved. My sobs turned into noiseless screams as the tears dried up and I bit my fist.

The door opened. James walked in and sat on the edge of my bed. He patted my leg. It was more of a comfort for me than anything Adam had done so far.

"I'm sorry, Selene. You did miscarry. I had the guys in the lab run a DNA test to confirm my theory. The baby was Adam's." James swiveled to look at Adam.

I rolled back onto my back so I could look at them both at the same time. The look Adam shot James seemed to say they had discussed this but Adam had not told me yet. James shrugged as if to say he was sorry.

I tried to sit up. Adam came to my aid despite my current state of selfishness. He used the mechanism on the bed to sit me upright. He propped a pillow up behind my head and covered me up with the seafoam green hospital blanket.

"What theory?" My voice came out clearer than it had before.

James turned away from my gaze. He didn't want to get in the middle of this relationship issue. It was the first sign of intelligent life I had seen in the vampire since I met him.

"Adam?" I slid my hand into his willing my eyes to stay open. I was just so tired.

"James thinks there is always a price to use magic. I used magic when I read from the *Book of the Dead* to transfer Baht's soul back to her body. The price I had to pay was our baby. She was the one thing in this world that was just mine and yours, the one thing we didn't have to share with Alexander." Adam gripped my hand tighter fighting the tears in his eyes.

149

"We were going to have a girl?" I didn't have the strength or the energy to stop the tears welling up in my eyes from falling. I felt like I was never going to stop crying and that it didn't matter if I did because I would be dead soon. When I died I wouldn't be able to cry anymore.

Adam hung his head. "It was too soon to tell. I was just hoping we were going to have a girl and that she took after her mother who is the single most amazing person I know."

Adam reached up to wipe my tears with his long shirt sleeve.

The door to my hospital room flung open hitting the door stopper hard enough to crack the base of the door. Sheriff Larry ran into the room. He was covered in blood.

"James, we need you in triage now." Larry didn't wait for James to acknowledge him. He ran out of the room at the same speed he had used to come in.

"I'm sorry, Selene. I have to go. I will come check on you later." James patted my leg again following Larry to triage.

"Adam," I turned to him slightly nauseous from all of the movement.

"I will go find out what happened." Adam leaned over and kissed my head.

"No, I mean, yes I want to know what happened. I was going to ask, I mean I wanted to know..." I was having a hard time finding the right words to ask him what I wanted to know because I was afraid of his answer.

Adam took my face in his hands and kissed me. "If you have eternity, so do I."

Adam left to find out why the Sheriff was covered in blood and what fresh horror awaited us when I could leave the hospital wing.

Chapter 20

Still reeling from my miscarriage, Sheriff Larry came back to my room with Adam. The Sheriff had copper colored blood drying at various rates covering almost every square inch of his uniform. Adam had some blood drying on his clothes too. Whatever had happened had been bad enough for Adam to feel the need to jump in and help or for the hospital staff to feel the need to ask Adam to jump in and help.

I put my hand up to stop Larry from explaining whatever it was he was going to explain. I didn't want excuses, I wanted answers. Specifically one answer.

"Who was it?"

The Sheriff rubbed his giant belly flaking dried blood off his uniform onto the tile floor, the shiny copper contrasted with the stark white of the tiles. "Some kind of attack. Harry and Lauren. We're still piecing together what happened. I'm sorry, Selene. Lauren didn't make it and Harry is barely hanging on."

Too many people had come into my hospital room today and apologized for things they had no control over. I felt bad that I had so much going on in my life that I hadn't even checked on Lauren after I died the first time. When I was a human, she had been my best friend. She had just married Harry. I guess some part of me thought she would be better off without me. Clearly, I was wrong. Whatever happened to them was supernatural in nature otherwise they wouldn't have been brought here. My last shred of humanity just died. There was nothing left to do now except kill as much evil as I could on my way to the Afterlife.

If I wasn't such a horrible friend I could have been there for Lauren and protected her from this. If I hadn't been such a terrible mother, I could have protected my daughter from the magic that took her away. I should have known that using magic, even if it was to right a wrong, would have a price. One that wouldn't be worth the cost. I also worried about the magic that bound Adam and I together. It was this magic that wouldn't let us stray far from the other. It was this magic that wouldn't let Alexander or the loss of our baby rip us apart. Magic always comes with a price. For magic this strong I hesitated to see what the price would be for us. I knew it would be far worse than anything that has happened so far.

"Larry, find Alexander." I closed my eyes unable to take the stress of the day any longer.

Chapter 21

I was released from the hospital wing a couple of days later. I was still in some pain. I thought that was a little unusual given the fact that I had died and come back to life so many times in the past. I guess since I didn't die this time my body wouldn't heal as quickly.

Adam told me that Harry survived the attack. They suspected werewolves from a pack nowhere near here that had moved on already. I was happy Harry was alive, but I couldn't bring myself to visit him. Not now. I had my own trauma to deal with. He also reminded me of Lauren and I wasn't ready to let her go. Not yet.

There had to be something in the *Book of the Dead* that could stop Alexander for good. I had a few ideas of things I would do to him once we found him. Trouble was, I needed magic for a lot of them and James wouldn't let me near the book. It didn't matter. Even if he would let me read it, I couldn't remember how to read a lot of hieroglyphs. It was a weird thing to lose after everything that had happened. I had basically lost my ability to read in my native language. No one had any suggestions as to why that happened. Baht was Egyptian too. It wasn't like she had the skill and I never did so I lost the ability when her soul left my body. It must have been tied to all of the other memories I couldn't remember even though my body was my own again.

One thing I did remember was Baht and I used to be friends. Until I killed her. With magic. Her soul in my body must have been the price I had to pay for using magic to do what I should have done with my bare hands. Her soul in my body was the reason for my memory loss, the reason why I didn't know myself anymore, the reason why I could barely remember my own mother's face. Her soul in my body was why my body did things without my permission. And I was the reason why her soul ended up in my body before I was done using it. All this time, I thought I was running from Baht and Alexander. Now, I knew I was really running from myself.

~

"Baht wake up." I was shaking Baht trying to get her to wake up without also waking up Alexander. Baht was notoriously difficult in all things especially waking from a deep sleep.

Baht rolled over away from Alexander. I used that as my opportunity to hold my hand over her mouth and pinch her as hard as I could. Her eyes shot open. I could hear her mumble a startled ouch and a 'what the hell' under my hand.

"Come on already," I removed my hand from her mouth and motioned for her to follow me.

Baht rolled her eyes regarding me as the little sister she never had or wanted. She followed me anyway.

I led her to a temple we reserved for honoring the dead.

"What are we doing here, Selene? I've never met any of these dead people." Baht was exasperated with my antics.

"You do know at least one of these dead people, Baht." I stopped at a dais in the back of the temple.

"Who do I know here?" Baht demanded. Her hands were rubbing up and down her arms. It was a chilly night and she hadn't dressed for getting out of bed.

"You." I began to read from a thick book with a gold cover.

In the space of time

When one shall live

154

The other shall die

How I had gotten ahold of the Book of the Dead I don't know. It didn't matter. I read from the book with purpose and an air of authority I'm sure I didn't possess at the time.

As I read from the book, Baht began to scream. It was agonizing to hear and worse to watch. Her body shriveled like it had been dead for a thousand years. I saw a black mass leave her body disappearing into the atmosphere. Before it was gone totally, Anubis arrived. He regarded me with the book like he had seen something shameful. He had. I had disrupted the natural order by using magic to kill Baht.

Anubis did his job as Ferrier of souls. He grabbed the tail of the black cloud that was Baht's soul and shoved the mass into a small gold orb. He walked over to the dais and took the Book of the Dead from me. I had used a spell to send a soul to the Underworld. Only, Baht wasn't dead and her soul was supposed to be in her body. Anubis went back to wherever he had come from. I went back to bed without thinking twice about having just killed a woman or what the price for my use of magic would be.

~

Now that I remembered why Baht and Alexander were pissed at me, I got a little pissed at myself. I had to have a reason for killing Baht like I did. That's the part I didn't remember. Her screams haunted me. I had repressed that memory of my own volition for a reason.

Adam still thought the death of our daughter was his fault. I knew it was mine. Everything that had happened to us these past two millennia were because I used magic to do something I should have done with my hands. Maybe. Maybe I shouldn't have killed her at all. I still wasn't sure why I wanted to kill her in the first place, only that I had used magic to do it.

If it had only been me who was being punished all this time, I wouldn't have felt so bad. Adam had to live through me leaving him time and time again to be with my brother. Adam had to live through me giving birth to a daughter with my brother then having to kill that

155

child because I couldn't. Adam was torn apart by a pack of hellhounds. Adam's soul was brought back from the Underworld causing him to roam the Earth for two hundred years thinking he was a monster no one would ever love. Adam lost the only child he had ever known. And now Adam was going to lose me. For good this time. The only way to keep him safe, to keep him from experiencing any more heartache was to break his heart one last time.

I found Adam in the library reading some kind of existentialist garbage trying to figure out his place in this world. I rolled my eyes. People like us didn't have a place anywhere except for the ones we created for ourselves, like Asylum. I looked into his impossibly blue eyes, faltering in my decision. I knew there would never be anyone else for me or anyone else for him. There was no way we could be apart for any length of time and not be miserable.

"Selene, good to see you out of bed. How are you feeling?" Adam pulled me down to his lap.

I couldn't do it. I couldn't be the one to break him. I was already a monster in my own right. I didn't need any help turning into something I used to hunt. "Better," I snuggled into him relishing in his unconditional love, a love I didn't deserve but craved so much.

Adam sighed. I knew he was thinking what I was thinking. This wasn't going to last. We wouldn't be able to spend the rest of our lives sitting in this chair together, never moving, never changing. Alexander would come for us. We could either wait for him to find us or we could find him first.

"Sheriff Larry is on it. After the attack on Lauren and Harry," my voice faltered again.

I still hadn't gone to see Lauren's body. I still hadn't asked Larry what he told her family. I still hadn't been to the medical wing to see Harry. I was still selfish. I was still a bad person. I was still determined to leave everyone I loved behind so I couldn't hurt them anymore. My only chance for redemption was stopping Alexander and our mother from destroying this world.

"After the attack on Lauren and Harry," I started again, "Larry upped all patrols both human and not. If there is anything weird going on in this town, it will be attributed to Alexander and we will find him. Until then, what do we do?" I knew Adam had a military type strategy that he was dying to employ here.

"I have already done some things such as order additional security and to change the routine here. He seems to have more information on us than we have on him. That makes him more dangerous than we are." Adam was talking low because we were still in the library. It didn't matter much. Vampires and werewolves have exceptional hearing. Everyone in the room was hanging on Adam's every word. I think he was telling me all of this to reassure them more than me.

"Now, he doesn't know our routines because you changed them all along with who guards what and how we get in and out?" I was confirming this more for me than for the eavesdroppers listening in.

"That's the idea." Adam closed the book he had been reading and set it on the end table on the right side of his chair.

"I can't sit in this underground prison forever." I sat up imploring him to agree.

"Didn't you say something like that to me a few months ago when I found you again after spending so much time without you?" Adam had a look that said he wasn't going to argue with me today.

I was tired of arguing too. I patted his knee and left before he could protest. I didn't know where I was going. I would figure it out when I got there.

Chapter 22

I found myself driving through a part of town I had never seen. As most things that have to do with magic go I had no idea how I ended up where I ended up or what I was supposed to do now that I was there. I wasn't going to find out sitting in the car though. I was parked in front of a seamstress shop. The trouble was when I squinted my eyes just right the seamstress shop turned into a witch's cottage.

Great. Witches are almost worse than demons. I wondered if there was a nice old hag who just liked to eat small children in there or if she was a melt your face for fun kind of bitch. Either way I knew I was going to have to kill her. That made me kind of happy. I was really jonesing to kill something. I probably didn't have the healthiest coping skills. Then again, I really didn't care.

I tucked some small knives into my shirt sleeves and my boots before walking into the shop. A little bell dinged above the door. Why did she need a bell if she was magic and knew I was there before I even pulled into the parking space?

"Oh, it's you." A plump woman with curly red orange hair wearing a stained apron over her dress greeted me. The stains on her apron were rust covered. I hoped it wasn't blood.

My right hand went to my hip unconsciously. "I'm always me. As hard as I try, I find it difficult to be anyone else." The events of the past week and my lack of sleep had left me less than pleasant. Who am I kidding? I'm never pleasant.

She frowned. "I wasn't expecting you for a few more days. She told me it would be at least Wednesday before you showed up."

"Who told you I was coming and ruined the surprise witch?" I took out one of the knives from my sleeve.

She sighed. "You have much to learn about the world you live in. I'm a light witch. I help while dark witches only hinder."

"If I have so much to learn then how can I be sure you aren't a dark witch saying some pretty words so I'll give you everything I have left? Which by the way isn't much." I took a step back from her right into a table of what I hoped were spices.

She rolled her yellow cat eyes at me. They didn't match her hair very well but I wasn't going to tell her that. "You can't. Trust me, I don't want your soul. It's too stained with the blood of the innocent. Madame Cosmescu did ask me to give this to you, so here it is. I did a summoning spell this morning to find it. I've already been paid so don't worry about that. Hurry along. The summoning spell will only last for three days before the spell turns sour and the magic runs out. When that happens, the box will make its way back to where I summoned it from." The witch was pushing me along trying to get me to leave her shop.

"Madame Cosmescu? The fortune teller? When did she ask you to do this for me?" I planted my feet using the door jamb for leverage.

"This morning. She did warn me you may be a problem." The witch was tying some strings from her apron pocket together.

"This morning? How? She's been dead for a month." I pushed her hands down trying to get her to pay attention to me.

"There's still a lot for you to learn. You should really try harder." She plucked a hair from my head and tied it to the stings in her hands.

I opened my mouth to protest. An unseen hand pulled me all the way back to my car.

I blinked in the new sunlight rising above the shops blinding me after being in the dark shop. When I could see again, I trudged back to the shop peering into the windows of the locked building. It was completely deserted and looked like it had been that way for some time. There was no witch's cottage or seamstress shop anymore. The whole strip mall was void of any people or businesses. The only way I could tell that whole experience had been real at all was the wood box laden with magic weighing heavily in my hands. I went back to the car feeling hot all over at being duped by an old hag and not getting to kill anything after the week I'd had.

I sat in the car letting the air conditioner blow on my face until I couldn't feel anything anymore. I stared at the box. It was locked. The witch hadn't given me a key. I fiddled with the box trying to figure out how to tell what was inside without being able to open it. I was just getting ready to run it over with my car when I found a small button. I pressed it without thinking. What could be the worst that could happen? Did it matter if something horrible happened? At this point in my life, nothing scared me anymore. I could tell from my newfound attitude this was the beginning of the end. Whose end I wasn't positive. I had a pretty good guess though.

A small tray lined in deep purple silk popped out of the bottom of the treasure box. The only thing inside was a small brass skeleton key. There were no distinguishing markings, writing or decorations. It was all very anti-climactic. I was kind of disappointed.

I used the key to open the box. Inside was a timeworn brass oil lamp. I shrugged to no one in particular, then pulled the lamp out of the protection of the box lined in the same dark purple silk as the drawer at the bottom.

Nothing.

I cracked the lid of the lamp closing one eye in case something popped out.

Nothing.

I tried frantically rubbing it like I had seen people do in movies a thousand times over.

Nothing.

Color me pissed off. This magic bullshit was such a waste of my time as always.

I threw the lamp and the box on the passenger seat and started the car. It wasn't until I checked my rear-view mirror to back out of my parking space that I noticed the guy in my back seat. I slammed on the brakes causing him to stir.

"I am Kazeem. Your wish is my command, master." His voice was velvet in my ear, smooth, sultry and rubbing me the right way.

Damn. My hormones must still be out of whack from my pregnancy. I couldn't sit here running my car in the parking lot of an abandoned building all day while a tall, sexy stranger stared at me making my arms prickle with goosebumps. I mean, I could stay here all day, I just shouldn't. Plus, what in the holy hell was I going to do with a genie? A tan, raven haired genie...

Fuck.

I shook my head clear of my wandering thoughts. I had a man I loved at home. My body was finally my own. I would eventually get over the death of my child to a point where Adam and I could try for another. Despite my crazy-ass homicidal mother still being on the loose, things were looking up for me. Why was I sabotaging myself? I was the reason why I couldn't have nice things. I was the reason why I could never be happy. Some part of me wondered if it was because deep down I knew all of the things that I had done and that I didn't deserve happiness. Another part of me wondered if I had never killed Baht and set this particular chain of events into motion if I would be happy or if it was in my nature to always be miserable. I kind of knew my answer. I can only be happy when miserable. It sounded counter-intuitive, but it was true. I relished in misery whether it was my own or other's. I was officially a terrible person.

The question I should have really asked myself at that point was did I want to continue being a terrible person or did I want to change. I didn't ask myself that at that particular moment and we all know I didn't change so...

Kazeem sat in my backseat with his arms folded across his chest. He made no sudden movements.

At first, I thought he must have known I had some type of weapon on me. After a few minutes of silence, it occurred to me that he and Anubis were far too alike. He was still and silent because he served a master. His job was to be neither seen nor heard until he was needed for whatever dumbass wish his current master needed him for.

What dumbass things should I wish for so I could get rid of him and get back to wallowing in the despair of my current situation?

I pulled my car back into the parking space I had been trying to vacate and shut off the engine. I tried to contort my body so I was face to face with Kazeem. The seatbelt I was wearing prevented such movements. I huffed. Why was everything so frustrating? Maybe I should make my first wish a sandwich. I was getting hangry. I flung the seatbelt off. The metal hook of the seatbelt hit the car window with a resounding thunk. I may have just created a claim for my car insurance company. I didn't care.

Whipping around to look Kazeem in the eyes instead of ogling him through my rearview mirror, I huffed again. "I knew I felt magic. What's your deal then? I get three wishes and you just go away?"

"Something like that. There are rules, though I see you already know. You have been touched by dark magic before." Kazeem stared into my eyes, his face expressionless.

"Yeah, well, no one ever explained the rules to me. Can you find and kill Alexander for me?" I had to make my first wish count for something and I was cool with a revenge killing at the moment.

"No, I am not allowed to harm anyone." His face remained stoic.

What else did I want? A fish and chips platter from *Gone Fishin'* sounded great right about now. I could get that on my own without too much effort. I wanted something that I would need both the Book of the Dead and a working understanding of hieroglyphics. Both of which I did not currently possess. Maybe this genie thing would be the next best thing.

I bit my lip. I didn't really want this wish, but it was the only way I could think of that would save him from the future I was creating for myself. "Can you make Adam forget me? Who I am? What I have done to him?"

Kazeem looked pained. His magic was old and ran deep. He knew what I was planning probably before I did. "No, this I cannot do for you. Soul magic is a magic I cannot break. You two have been entwined for more years than I have the strength to erase."

"What good are you then?" I started crying.

Kazeem patted my shoulder and handed me a piece of cloth. I blew my nose on it. I didn't care what it was or that it smelled like pipe tobacco and saw dust. His touch was warm and calming. "Can you fix my life at all?"

"Only you can fix your life as you are the only one who feels it is broken." Kazeem was still patting me on the shoulder. "I cannot do what you ask, however, I can offer some advice."

I looked up meeting Kazeem's clear dark brown eyes with my red puffy ones.

"Trust Adam to be an asset in your coming battle not a limitation. I think you will be pleasantly surprised by the way your souls respond to each other in combat."

I wiped my nose one more time before I handed back his swatch of cloth. Kazeem took the cloth and put it back in his pocket. I guess he didn't have any regard for laundry.

I still had three wishes and no clue what to wish for. I guess I could keep the lamp for a couple of days, but the red-haired witch said the spell would go south soon. If I wanted to use my wishes, it was kind of now or never. Madame Cosmescu clearly wanted me to have these wishes to do something. What was she trying to tell me? Maybe there was a way I could ask her.

Clarity of thought brightened my demeanor. "Kazeem, can you summon a ghost?"

Kazeem closed his eyes. His face scrunched like he was fighting a migraine and I was the cause. "I can certainly try. Spiritualization is a delicate art. Whom would you like to summon?"

"Madame Luiza Cosmescu."

"If you wish it so, I will do your bidding, Master."

"I wish to speak with the spirit of Madame Luiza Cosmescu right now."

"Your wish is my command." Kazeem's arms were still folded. He seemed to be concentrating too hard. His body jerked then grew still.

I was reaching out to touch Kazeem to check on him when a thin shape began to form in my passenger seat. Mitch materialized before my eyes.

"Dammit, Kazee!, I asked for this jerk's grandma not this jerk. I don't want to talk to him." I thumbed toward Mitch's spirit now haunting my car.

Kazeem's eyes were still closed. He didn't answer me.

"Selene, please. I'm sorry. Alexander didn't exactly give us a choice."

I turned away from Kazeem to scowl at the ghost in my passenger seat. "There is always a choice, Mitch. You could have come to me. I would have helped you. Instead, you let a demon inhabit your body and tried to kill me. More importantly, I had to be the one to hold your grandmother's hand while she died. That wasn't my place. The two of you should never have been involved in my business to begin with. I can't keep being the one to watch the people around me die knowing I'm the cause of their suffering." I folded my arms and turned to look out the driver's side window.

"I convinced Bunica to let me come instead. I had to tell you how sorry I am. Alexander told me if I didn't let that demon use my body he would kill my grandmother. You don't understand. She was all I had left." Mitch tried to touch my arm. His spirit couldn't latch on. As his hand fell through my body, the look on his face fell along with it. "My grandmother wanted me to tell you that if you really want Adam to forget you for eternity you have to ask Kazeem for the *Book of the Dead*. There is a spell in there that will help you."

I turned back toward Mitch. He was a cute kid when he wasn't trying to kill you. He looked all of eighteen years old. He was too young to die, especially how he did. Demon or not, it must have hurt to have Sheriff Larry's slugs rip him apart from the inside out until his entire body disintegrated.

I regarded Mitch with a quiet contemplation I hadn't before (probably because he had been trying to kill me the last time I saw him). "I thought of that already. It doesn't matter if I have the book. I can't remember enough of my past life to read it properly."

I went back to staring out the window frustrated by my incompetence as a person and my inability to use a genie to my advantage in what would surely end up being an all-out war for humanity. If I let my mother win, whatever she and her merry band of misfits had in mind for the rest of the world would not be in their best interests. I was imaging some type of global pharaoh that killed the unworthy and that was me not even trying. I'm sure what Cleopatra actually had in mind was much worse.

"Selene," Mitch whined. "You have two wishes left. Ask for the book and all of your memories. Be careful though. If you ask for your memories, you won't just get the ones you made in your body, you will also have returned the memories of the things Baht did in your body." Mitch tried to touch my arm again. He still couldn't. "I really am sorry, Selene."

Mitch faded away into nothingness. Kazeem opened his eyes in the backseat clearly over whatever magic he had to use to bring Mitch back to me. Despite the betrayal, I still appreciated seeing Mitch again. He seemed like a nice kid when he wasn't inhabited by a demon.

He was also right. If I wished for my memories back, I would re-gain the knowledge to read hieroglyphs. I shuddered. What did I do that was so bad it made me forget how to read in my native language in the first place? I still hesitated to make the wishes. What if the things I remembered left me unable to function? Baht and Mitch both made me sound like a monster before I started being controlled by Baht's soul. What if I had been a monster? What if my memories made me want to go back to that life? Would I? Could I be that person all over again?

I guess it didn't matter much in the long run. I had to do *something* and making these wishes was the only thing I could think to do.

I turned back to Kazeem in the backseat. He hadn't shifted from his standard operating position of straight backed sitting with his arms folded across his chest. "Kazeem, I wish for you to give me the *Book of the Dead*."

"As you wish, master." Kazeem unfolded his arms. A thick book bound in gold leather appeared in his hands. He handed the book to me.

I opened it to make sure it was the right book. As far as I could tell it was.

I made my last wish based on the recommendations of a guy I still didn't know I could totally trust but who was the only one in this car at the moment making any sense. "Kazeem, for my last wish, I wish to recover all of my memories."

"As you wish, Master." Kazeem blinked disappearing into a cloud of smoke and fog.

I opened the *Book of the Dead* to see if I could read it now that my memories had been recovered.

"What the holy fucking shit is this?" I threw the book back on the passenger seat before banging my forehead against the steering wheel.

I still couldn't read the hieroglyphs. Come to think of it, I hadn't had any other profound revelations from returned memories either. Was the retrieval of memories something that came with time? When Kazeem left, I thought a rush of wind would rock the car and I would just have everything I have been wanting since I found out who I really was.

I fucking hate magic. I didn't have time to recover these memories slowly. I was surprised my mother hadn't attempted to kill me since she sent Mitch to make sure my body never left the morgue. For a supposed immortal, time was not on my side.

I tried rubbing Kazeem's lamp to see if I could get him to come out and talk to me. I didn't need more wishes, I needed clarity. He didn't re-appear. I put his lamp back in the box and locked it. I hid the key in the secret compartment before dropping the whole thing in a charity donation bin. Then, I headed home to break what I had just fixed right before I left. If I couldn't use the *Book of the Dead* to make Adam forget me, I would break his heart the old fashioned way.

Chapter 23

I turned left instead of right. I don't know why I did it. I had my right blinker on. I tried to turn my car around but my body and my mind weren't on the same page. It was like Baht was controlling my body and I was aware of everything that was happening. My chest felt tight. I was having a hard time breathing.

I concentrated on breathing in and then breathing out. I didn't have to concentrate on driving. It didn't matter if I crashed. I couldn't die.

In.

Out.

Okay, I was feeling less controlled by someone else. I looked out the driver side window. Cows. I looked out the passenger side window. Houses. I knew where my body was going against my will. I wondered if this had anything to do with the wish I had made to recover my memories. Kazeem had said my wish was his command but I hadn't recovered any memories at the time. He didn't seem like he could go back on his word even if he wanted to. Whatever magic bound him to his bottle bound him to his word.

I turned left at the gas station/post office combo I passed by the last time I went to Eternal Life Church. I kept driving until I reached a dirt road almost completely hidden by trees and bushes. Despite the fact that I couldn't die, I was glad I was wearing my seatbelt. As soon as my tires went from paved road to dirt road the impact jostled me in my seat making me bounce up toward the ceiling.

I debated turning off my headlights when I reached the eerie church. What hunted me would surely find me either way. I left my headlights shining on the church graveyard hoping no one was in the church, though I had the prickly hairs on your neck feeling that someone was watching me.

There was a young girl in a colonial dress sobbing soundlessly by a headstone that read Adelaide. I couldn't make out the last name. It was too worn down by time. I knew how the headstone felt. I was too worn down by time myself. My head felt full and my eyelids heavy. I wanted to lay my head on the lap of the crying girl and let her comfort me even though I should be the one comforting her. She was the one crying after all.

I trudged through unkempt gravesites stumbling every so often as I made my way to the girl. I touched her on the shoulder. My headlights went out. I flipped out. I knew I was supposed to be something akin to a goddess hunter who took out bad guys like a boss, but I was no good with total darkness. There could be too many things out there trying to touch me. Like snakes. I did not do snakes. Not after last time.

A now familiar hand over my mouth stifled my screams. Maybe my lack of sleep had finally rotted out the inside of my skull leaving everything I needed a pile of cold grey goo. When I realized the hand belonged to the man I had been planning to kill, I relaxed. He would have killed me in the darkness as soon as my headlights went out if that was what he aimed to do. Alexander took his hand off my mouth and fireman carried me to another row of graves in a clearing. There was a perfect blackness lingering in the air that could only be achieved by a moonless night.

"The dreams don't stop for you either, do they, sister?" I could barely make out Alexander's shadow. It was only slightly inkier than the dark that surrounded us.

"I guess I'm just not that lucky."

We were whispering. I didn't know why. We were in the dark and whispering was what people did in the dark. There was no one around to hear what we were talking about. Well, no one except for Adelaide. I doubted as a ghost she cared very much about, well, very much.

"Must be a family trait." He whispered gruffly before snorting.

"I'm sorry, you know, for killing Baht in the first place and for now, for taking her away from you again." I touched his arm actually feeling something for my brother that I hadn't in a long time.

"I'm sorry too, though not for what I have already done, only for what I am about to do." Alexander grabbed me by the throat with both of his hands. He was trying to choke me.

I clawed at his face and hands trying to get him off of me. Alexander was lifted away from my body by something I couldn't see. I heard a tree snap in half as Alexander's body hit the tree's trunk. God, I hoped it wasn't a bear or something large and paranormal. I didn't want to deal with that right now.

A car horn beeped in the darkness at the same time headlights flickered. Another car was here with us. Another car with its trunk now open. In the dim flashes of light, I could see Adam. He had come for me just like he always had in the past. He was carrying Alexander's unconscious body back to his car. It didn't matter if we defeated Alexander together right here, right now, Adam would be better off if he just forgot about me for the rest of eternity. Wouldn't he?

"What are you doing here? I had that situation completely under control. I don't need you saving me all the time." I was trying to follow Adam back to the cars on the hill. I kept tripping over the same brush and undergrowth I had tripped over a few minutes ago before Alexander carried me to the clearing.

Adam didn't say anything for a long time. He left me alone with my thoughts making me go to a dark place real fast. The graveyard air was suffocating me. I was having another panic attack worse than the one I had in the car on the way here. My life was spiraling out of control. Then, the voices started whispering my name.

~

Someone grabbed my arm. I was transported to a densely wooded forest where I could see a small castle in the distance. I was following myself on a path I knew well. I turned around to stare back at me.

"Who are you?" I was shouting at the woman. I hadn't meant to or needed to. The words just sort of came out that way in my fit of panic.

The woman turned around fully to stare at me. She was a me from a different time period. She- I mean I- was wearing a black corset laced so tightly my breasts looked like cannonballs shoved under some sheer fabric. I had a skirt that went to my ankles and fingerless gloves that went to my elbows. I immediately hated the clothes from this time period on me. I looked ridiculous.

Past me put a finger to my lips. Present me turned around. It was just us in the forest. Where were we? How did past me know I was there? This was a memory, wasn't it? It had to be. We heard the voices calling my name, our name, again.

The other me put her hand up stopping me. I crouched down behind a thick fallen log. Past me went toward the voices.

Alexander was there with a red-haired woman. The woman almost looked like me if I would have dyed my hair fire engine red. Alexander grabbed the me from the past and threw her into a coffin sealing it with nails. I could hear her banging on the lid trying to get out. I rushed from behind the log to help her. I tried to grab Alexander's arm and fell through. The red-haired companion stared right at me. She looked like me because she was my mother. She was almost completely unrecognizable with her hair dyed that way.

"Stop shouting, Selene. No one can hear you." My mother leaned down to talk to my coffin, the same coffin she was going to use to bury me alive.

171

"Mom, does Selene's need to die so we can raise dad from the Underworld?" Alexander was whining at my mother's side like a two year old asking for candy before dinner.

"Dammit, Alexander! Unless I can get the Book of the Dead from her, she has to die before your father can come back. I need to trade her soul for his." Cleopatra pushed Alexander away from her. "Selene's soul can rot in Underworld prison for the next two thousand years. I need your father back so I can rule this world."

"Mom! You said I could have Selene's body to do what I wanted. This is so unfair!" Alexander was full on pouting now. He was sitting on my coffin with his arms folded and his bottom lip jutting out.

The air before me grew thick until it turned dark again.

~

I was back in the graveyard breathing in and out shakily waiting for the next ghost to take hold of me. Adam was standing over me. I didn't see Alexander. I could see the faint pinks and oranges rising above the trees. Trees that looked familiar. Past me from my latest escapade into my repressed memories stood before me baring her neck. There were puncture marks from vampire teeth and claw marks from lycanthropes running the length of her body down into her dress. Had I died that night? Unclear. If I had, my soul never made it to the Underworld. Past me dissolved as the first few rays of the sun washed over the cemetery.

I think I was starting to understand. Not only was my mother still alive somewhere but she had orchestrated this whole nightmare I had been living in just so I would marry my brother and keep the royal bloodlines pure. Marrying Cassius was a ruse to get me to kill myself so my mother could use my body against my permission. When my body was hers, she would be able to take anything she wanted from the rest of the world. With my soul gone, she would be able to trade me for my father.

"What happened? Where did you go without me?" Adam was holding me, smoothing my hair, talking low, doing all of the things I would miss if I made him forget me.

172

"I found a way to get my memories back. I think that is what is happening now." I looked over his shoulder. He turned his head to see what I was concerned with.

Adelaide was still here. She had finally stopped crying. She watched me intently as another woman, who could have been mistaken for me from behind, sauntered up to me. I didn't wait for my memory to grab me and violently transport me to another time in the life of the graveyard. I climbed out of Adam's lap and grabbed her hand first.

~

I was at a dance club. It was Grace's bachelorette party. Grace was an acquaintance of mine from Marcus's pack in the city. Grace and I were both surprised when I showed up at her bachelorette party uninvited. Once enough drinks flowed through our veins, Grace didn't care that the woman who turned down her fiancé was there. I don't know why I was there or how I knew about the bachelorette party. I hoped Grace and Marcus would be happy together. I wasn't even angry I didn't get a wedding invite.

Grace and I were dancing with pink drinks in our hands. We didn't have enough cloth covering us to constitute as clothing in any world other than the club scene. Some of Grace's cousins and friends from the pack were standing by the bar probably being catty bitches like they normally were.

"I love this song," I shouted to Grace. There would be no quiet conversations in this place, the DJ made sure of that.

Grace danced closer to me. A shadow passed her face making it look strange. I was drunk and I knew it. I wrote it off as blue strobe lighting not being Grace's color. The lighting came back around, red this time, and flashed on something in Grace's hand. It was hard to tell what it was. It didn't look like her drink glass.

It was too late for me to block the first thrust of the ceremonial onyx blade in Grace's right hand. It was also too late for me to register that Grace was left handed. My movements were slowed by alcohol and by a betrayal from someone I considered to be my friend. I knew I had a loose definition of the word friend but this was ridiculous.

By the third thrust of Grace's blade, I was becoming myself again. I had two stab wounds in vital places. Idiot club-goers danced around us thinking we were dancing, either because they were too drunk or too stupid to realize what was really going on. My vote was stupidity. I blocked another stab wound to my intestines with my arm. The blade went through the skin of my outer arm through the bone and out the other side in to my abdomen. The blow to my abdomen was not as severe as my other stab wounds but my arm was definitely broken. I heard the bone shatter over the sound of music blaring so loud no one heard my screams for help.

I kept hitting Grace in places she should have been vulnerable. I hit her on the side of her head with my drink spraying glass all over us making the floor slick with alcohol that mixed with my blood that already coated the tile in a layer just thin enough for us to slide on in our high heels. She didn't get a scratch on her. I punched her in the face and in the stomach. She didn't flinch once. All I could do at this point was block my vital organs and hope someone helped me.

I looked over to where the rest of the bridal party was holed up. It hadn't been their idea to come to this club. They wanted to sit at a quiet bar downtown. It had been my idea. Grace had latched on to the whole plan like a kid holding on to the doors of a candy store. That should have clued me in that something was wrong. Grace would never go out dancing at a club like this.

The bridal party parted revealing Grace sitting on a bar stool crying. How could she be crying over there if she was busy stabbing me over here? I looked back to the person in front of me. The girl stabbing was no longer Grace.

"Took you long enough, Selene. Even with all of the alcohol you consumed tonight, you should have known it was me." The woman staring back at me had on less clothes than I remembered her wearing when she was pretending to be Grace. She also had a black bob and a scarab amulet on a chain around her neck. It looked like a smaller version of the bracelet I had stolen from her just before she faked our deaths.

174

My mother pushed me to the floor of the club straddling me. She stabbed me over and over spraying my blood in her mouth and eyes.

And I let her.

~

I was back to present time in the graveyard. Adelaide took my hand. I braced myself wondering where she would take me next. She stared at me intently. We had gone nowhere. "Those weren't ghosts, were they?"

She shook her head.

"They were my memories? These are the things I was trying so hard to forget? These are the things I wished for when I asked Kazeem to restore my life to me?" I was frowning at her hoping she wouldn't confirm what I had been thinking and wondering why I had such an affinity for trusting the people that I loved even when I knew the evil they were capable of.

Adelaide was about five inches shorter than me which was a feat given that I was only five feet tall. "Yes."

Adam was shaking me. I could hear and see him. I couldn't feel him near me. It was like both Adelaide and I were in the spirit world. Adelaide must have needed me here with her for some reason.

"What happened to you?" I looked down at her whispering my question unsure if I wanted to know the answer. She seemed too sweet for something brutal and gruesome to have happened to her.

"You killed me a long time ago when a demon took over my body. Don't you remember?" Adelaide cocked her head to the side like a dog waiting for a bone.

I tried to hug her only getting armfuls of air. "I'm sorry. I wish I remembered you."

"That's what you're here for. To remember." Adelaide grabbed my arm tighter than I was comfortable with. Her hand didn't pass

175

through me like I had passed through her when I tried to hug her a moment ago.

Adelaide held both of my arms behind my back. I couldn't get away. Shadows appeared before me. The shadows were shaped like people. I couldn't make out their faces but I knew they were unhappy with me.

"Meet are all of the people you killed in your lifetime. They will help you remember." Adelaide let my arms go. I couldn't move. Something rooted me to my spot in the cemetery.

I was paralyzed by fear and shame. There were so many of my ghosts here and I couldn't remember a single one. In a wave of emotion, all of the ghosts that had been chasing me my entire life finally caught up to me. I closed my eyes. I couldn't watch them hurt me like I had hurt them. I deserved it. I knew I did.

I let them come.

When I opened my eyes, I was still in the graveyard being cradled in Adam's arms. He was cradling me with one arm rocking back and forth. Adelaide stood behind him looking like she had when I first pulled up to the graveyard. I screamed meaning to warn Adam. Nothing came out of my mouth.

Adelaide frowned like she didn't understand why I was so upset. "Shame you keep getting too tangled up in what's not important to figure out what is. Shame it's taking you so long to break this curse that your misery has lasted centuries beyond what any one person should have to endure." Adelaide disappeared leaving me to put the pieces of my life back together on my own.

If I trusted the memories the cemetery returned to me, I thought maybe I was screwed. I left myself relax at Adam's touch.

Breathe in.

Breathe out.

I tried it a few times. Good. I could still do it on my own. I stood up lending Adam a hand so he would come with me.

"Selene?" Adam started to ask me if I was okay but thought better of it. Instead, he tucked some errant strands of hair back behind my ear.

"I'm going to be fine." I held his hand as we picked our way to the first line of gravestones. I stopped at Adelaide's grave to clear it. I wanted to do something nice for her since it was my fault she was dead. There was no grave marker with the name Adelaide. I dropped Adam's hand running down every row, picking myself up every time I fell on underbrush and broken grave markers.

I searched the whole graveyard thinking I had the wrong row, the wrong place in line. I didn't. No one named Adelaide was laid to rest there, at least not any place that was marked. I knew I hadn't driven all the way out here to make something like this up. I could have invented these visions from the safety of my bed had I been so inclined. I was not that inclined. I was also not inclined to keep standing in a haunted graveyard pondering my own existence and my future, full sun rise or not.

"Selene, whatever is going on, we can fix it, just not right now. Alexander will be waking up soon. I'd like to get him back to Asylum first." Adam was imploring me to give up the ghost literally and he didn't even realize it.

Alexander.

I stormed over to Adam's car. "Open it," I commanded.

He looked like he wanted to argue and wasn't sure he should. The trunk opened. Alexander sprang out on the offensive. I was ready for him this time. All of the fear and anger that had been building up all these years was finally remembered.

And I was pissed.

Alexander was still in mid-air when I grabbed the front of his shirt throwing him to the ground. I got on top of him and started punching as hard and as fast as I could. I didn't care if I hurt him or if I only hurt me in the process. I really just wanted to punch something and he was it. Alexander had his arms up guarding his face. I didn't care. I didn't stop until Adam pulled me off of Alexander.

"Selene, that's enough." Adam held me until I calmed down.

He ripped the hem of his t-shirt using the scraps of fabric to wrap my hands. They were raw and bloody. And aching with satisfaction. Alexander laid on the ground with his purple bruised arms raised still protecting his face. There were patches of blood all over his arms that made him look like he had a rash. I knew that was my blood. I stopped caring about my brother when the first ghost from my past told me what he and my mother had done, what they were still planning to do.

I went to my car and got the *Book of the Dead* from the front passenger seat.

"Where did you get that? James has that locked up in a place so secret even I don't know where it is." Adam tried to take the book from me. I didn't let him.

I began to read from the book. It was the same spell I used to kill Baht. I was going to use it to kill Alexander.

In the space of time

When one shall live

"Selene, no!" Adam was trying to get me to stop. I wasn't going to.

Alexander's body started to dehydrate and shrivel. It gave me a sick satisfaction knowing he would go to the Underworld to be judged. There was no way he wasn't going to some part of hell that would actually make him think twice about obeying our mother. Then again, why send him to hell when I could give him everything he ever wanted?

I stopped the spell before Alexander's soul left his body. He didn't re-hydrate. He stayed a shriveled shell of a man. Like he wasn't a shell of a man before.

I started to drag Alexander's almost corpse to my car. Adam stopped me.

"Selene, this isn't you. Stop for a minute. Let's figure this out." Adam had his hand on my shoulder.

"Don't you see, Adam? This *is* who I am. I have everything figured out. You can either help or get out of the way." I brushed Adam's hand off my shoulder and started dragging Alexander's body to my car again.

"I can't let you do whatever it is you are about to do. Your soul belongs to me and mine to you. I will not let you tarnish it."

"Please let me go, Adam. You will be better off. Your soul will be better off."

"If you've got eternity so do I."

"Maybe neither of us should have eternity then." I opened the book to a part I knew well. Adam would forget me. I would make sure of it.

Omit from conscious memory

Your one true love

For all of eternity

Never to know one another

Throughout the space of time again

Adam fell to the ground beside Alexander. I ran to check his pulse. I hadn't meant to kill him. I only wanted him to forget I ever existed and that we were ever married and that we had a daughter taken from us because I couldn't stand the mournful looks and the sideways glances any more. Adam's pulse was strong. I watched as his eyes danced behind closed lids.

I wondered briefly what else Adam forgot besides me, even though I didn't really have the time to stand around worrying about him. I also wondered if forgetting me meant forgetting Alexander and our situation too. I hadn't told him about finding out my mother's plan. I hadn't had a chance to tell anyone yet. I realized I might actually need Adam to help me figure out and foil my mother's plan. From what I gathered during one of my returned memories, my father was imprisoned in the Underworld and only a soul trade could free him. Once freed, I wondered what havoc he and my mother would wrought on the world. She has always wanted to rule more than what she had. That was one of the reasons why Octavian had tried and succeeded in taking over our lands so long ago.

I remembered the coin I kept in my pocket. One side had my mother's face and the other a man I did not know. I wondered if he was my father. Even with all of my memories recovered, I didn't know who my father was. I'm not sure I ever did.

I used to believe I was the fatal cure for evil. As I drug Alexander to my car, I wondered who would cure me. It took some doing. I got Alexander's semi-corpse into the backseat of my car. Muscles I didn't even know I had were on fire begging me for the sweet release only alcohol could bring. I didn't have time for that now. I threw the *Book of the Dead* in the front passenger seat taking the only road in and out of the little town cursed by my very existence.

Chapter 24

I don't know if it was a mistake to call James from the road or not. When I got back to Vampireville the strike team was waiting in the parking lot with a gurney. I hastily put the *Book of the Dead* in my purse and got out to meet them.

"He's in the back. Be careful, boys, he's damaged goods." I stepped out of the way waving the strike team over to my car.

Gary peered into my backseat before opening the car door. He let out a long whistle. "Selene, you are the reason why we can't have nice things." Gary chuckled.

"Don't I know it?" I slapped Gary on the back keeping a watchful eye on my brother.

One thing I omitted from my phone call with James, was the fact that my mother was the one who killed me. I don't know why I couldn't bring myself to tell anyone. We suspected she was the reason why I was in the morgue that night. I just wasn't ready to say those words out loud yet, to tell anyone what she had done to me, to say out loud what I planned to do to her.

James stepped into the parking lot from the shadow of the side of the building. "A request has been made that I have decided to honor. Put him on a gurney and take him to the same room we are keeping Baht's sarcophagus." James had a sour look on his face like he had just stepped in dog vomit. He didn't right his frown before waltzing back in the building.

I followed him trying to keep up. I made it to the entrance when I heard some of the strike team guys call Adam's name. Double shit. This was going to go poorly no matter which way it went down. Either Adam was going to remember me and be pissed or he was going to forget me and James would be pissed. Someone was always pissed at me these days.

I ran into the building at about the same speed James had walked earlier. Have I mentioned how much I hate running? Have I also mentioned how good Reginald was at scaring the crap out of me unnecessarily? That's exactly what he did when he stepped in front of me as I used the library entrance. I collided with his small, sturdy frame. He didn't flinch. I, however, almost fell over backward. Reginald grabbed my arm to keep me from disgracing myself in front of every single person who knew Asylum existed. The entire world seemed to have heard about the capture of Alexander and came out to see him for themselves.

Everyone crammed into the library started clapping. I knew it wasn't because Reggie kept me from falling over. I turned around. Adam was leading the strike team guys as they paraded Alexander's body through Asylum. Reggie stepped aside pulling me with him. We watched Alexander glide by on a metal gurney from the morgue. I guess James took the word corpse literally because I had thrown it around several times during our conversation. My mouth had been moving just as fast as my car had been speeding down what constituted as a highway in this town.

I followed the gurney careful to stay out of Adam's line of sight. I didn't want to deal with him right now. Or ever again if I could help it. I figured that was now impossible since he found his way out of the graveyard and back to Vampireville. At least he hadn't forgotten everything about his life. Just me.

"There she is. Selene, come over here." James ushered me into the secure room that housed Baht and all of her accoutrements.

"James, I'd like to be alone with my brother." I turned so Adam couldn't see my face fully, only my profile.

For a second, I had the thought that I hoped he wouldn't think I was fat seeing me from the side like that. Then, I remembered it wasn't my place to worry about what he thought of me or any other woman for that matter. I knew Adam not remembering me was not my consequence for using magic on him. That was the purpose of the magic spell I had so hastily cast. I didn't have time to think about how the world would screw me all over again and again for using magic this time, especially since it was an ancient magic according to Kazeem. I didn't have anything left for magic to take as payment in kind. And, I was about to use magic one more time to punish Alexander like he had punished me.

"I'm sorry. Have we met?" Adam used my shoulder to turn my body around so I could face him.

I wasn't ready to face him. I didn't ever want to face him again. My face burned with the shame of what I had done. "No, I don't think so." I brushed his hand off my body feeling electrified where he touched me. I was pissed my body was betraying me in the worst way. I turned back to James. "Can I get a minute alone with Alexander or not?"

"Selene," James started but never finished. "Sure. Adam, let's you and I go into my office to talk while Selene has her moment." James walked out of the secure room motioning to the strike team guys guarding the inside to exit with him.

Adam took one last long look at me before shaking any thoughts of us out of his head.

I turned my back on the window into the secure room so I wouldn't be seen by the guards. I pulled out the *Book of the Dead* to complete my spell. "Alex, I really need you to man up and tell me where mom is. It's kind of important. In return, I will restore your body."

I put my face close to Alexander's. I couldn't tell if the death I was smelling was coming from him or me. I could feel the darkness of my soul leeching out through my pores. I had to keep it together for a little while longer to do what needed to be done. I would never find rest until I stopped my mother.

183

Alexander's eyes fluttered behind his lids. Sounds emanated from his gullet like he was trying to speak to me. I said the spell to animate Alexander's corpse hoping he would tell me something useful. Alexander's skin stayed shriveled hugging all of the bones in his body. The only difference was now his mouth moved. It took all I had not to sew it shut.

"You little bitch! How could you do this to me? When mom finds you she's going to kill you." Alexander was screaming obscenities and truths at me. I didn't want to hear either.

I put my hand over his mouth. I turned my head to see if the guards were looking. They weren't. I knew I didn't have much time. "Listen to me you little shit. If you help me, I will help you. If you try to fuck me over like you have been my whole life, I will end you. Do you understand?"

Alexander nodded his head. I moved my hand.

"I don't know where she is. I've never known where she was. Mom always contacted me." It was hard to track Alexander's eye movements. Only his eyes and his mouth were moving. His eyes were moving faster than his mouth distracting me, making it hard to keep up with what he was saying.

I could have used another spell from the book to torture him into telling me where mom was. I didn't have to though. I could always tell when Alexander was lying to me. Today was no different. He didn't know. I flipped through the book finally finding what I was looking for. I couldn't use the spell Adam used earlier to get Baht's soul out of my body because Alexander didn't have two souls in his body. I had nothing entangled to untwine.

I had to use the spell Alexander had inadvertently used to curse me with a second half-life. He's always been a moron. Even our tutor said so, when I was still alive and allowed to go to school, when I was still alive and not betrothed to my brother. A bitter substance made its way from my stomach into my mouth. I tasted alkaline and rust. I fought the urge to gag swallowing hard. I started the spell.

Two suns joined by darkness

Living in perpetuity

Alexander's corpse stopped animating. Alexander's corpse stopped screaming. I watched his soul, black as a moonless night, seek freedom from his body. I knew the strike team guys were behind me watching the aftermath of what I had done. I knew James was not far away and not pleased either. I also knew that when my soul finally left my body it would be the same inky darkness hellhounds were made of. Compared to mine, Alexander's soul should have been nominated for sainthood.

James was breathing down my neck. I could feel his hot air trying to smother me from behind. I couldn't concentrate on anything except my brother. His soul found the place I had sent it when I read the spell. Baht's sarcophagus opened of its own accord. When Alexander's soul infiltrated her body, Baht's corpse screamed. I knew firsthand how unpleasant it was to have two souls in the same body. I hoped they would be happy together trapped in her corpse for eternity. I knew I would be happy in any dark hole James deigned to put me in knowing that Baht was torturing my brother forever.

Since I got my memories back, I realized it was just like me to let someone else do my dirty work for me. I smiled at the knowledge I had finally gotten almost everything I wanted in life. I kept smiling as James took the *Book of the Dead* back from me, leading me away from the secure room and the tormented souls of my enemies.

Chapter 25

I didn't resist. Half of the Vampireville strike team led me to the same cells where I used to question prisoners and calm down new wolves. Vampire Jail. I deserved everything I got and then some. Not now. Not yet. I still had justice to met out. My mother would be hard to find on my own. I needed a plan.

"Selene, are you listening?" James turned around sharply staring me down from above the shoulders of Garrison and Marks.

My two favorite strike team guys turned to face me. Marks shook his head. He still couldn't believe he was escorting someone to vampire jail that he had been in combat with a few days before. Garrison wasn't disappointed in me so much as super pissed. He kept pushing me along like I wasn't already walking on my own.

I kept walking, ignoring James and all of his questions. I had heard him. I didn't know what my plan was until I did it. I didn't know where Alexander was until he found me. I didn't know how to read the spells in the *Book of the Dead,* let alone use them, until I got my memories back.

"I used a genie to wish for my memories back. I'm not sorry, you know. About any of it." I had turned back briefly to address James before finding my way through three security checkpoints to a six foot by six foot cell in the lower depths of Vampireville.

"Selene, you are not making any sense. Let me help you." James was exasperated by my actions.

I couldn't exactly blame him for not understanding where I was coming from, but I needed everyone I ever knew to stay away from me. They were safer that way. Even James, a man I detested only slightly less than my brother. Maybe after I had done what was needed, I could explain things to the people in my life who ever loved me, I could re-build all of the bridges I was burning right now.

I walked into my prison cell of my own accord and closed the barred door behind me. If I was going to be punished, it would be on my own terms. I would follow my mother's example. When Octavian came for her, she locked herself in her living quarters and took her own life. I wasn't ready to go that far. I still had a lot to do before I died one last time, but if I was starting my descent into the Underworld, I would act every bit of the queen I was born to be on the way down.

James was standing by the door of my cell disapproving of my life choices when every alarm Vampireville ever created for any reason went off. Lights of various colors meaning various things strobed throughout the entirety of Vampireville. The red strobes meant fire, the blue mean a breech in our outer defenses and the white meant something important I couldn't remember. Maybe the pope died. I don't know. It's not like I actually read the manual they gave me when I was forced to live here. Come to think of it, none of the alarms had ever gone off (not even for testing) while I was tenured here.

The noise the alarms made was the worst of it. Maybe if only one alarm was going off it wouldn't be so bad. All of the alarms were going off at once and the decibel level being thrust upon us was deafening for me in the small concrete jail space. I couldn't imagine how the shifters and vampires felt with their heightened senses. All of the strike team guards who brought me in were humans with advanced combat training. They were fine. The guards who regularly babysat the jail were all some type of supernatural and were all holding their ears.

I put my hands over my ears and shouted to James, "What the hell is going on?"

James was too dignified to hold his ears like a toddler with an ear ache despite his heightened vampire senses. "Internal alarms were just triggered. We only have them on-"

James didn't bother to finish his sentence before he bolted out of vampire jail with enough speed to ruffle my hair during his odd exit.

I stood there, in my jail cell, with the palms of my hands blocking the noise from my ears for at least another five minutes before the alarms were turned off. The strobe lights remained on for a few more minutes before the reset switch was flipped turning them off as well.

I paced my cell for a few minutes trying to give my jailers a break from their recent sensory overload before I couldn't take it anymore. "What was that? Where did James go?"

A ghost drifted in through the outer jail door. He looked like he was about nine years old when he died. He had on a page boy hat with a thin brim and he was carrying a newspaper. I craned my neck to see what his newspaper said.

New York Bulletin, March 10, 1917

Dog Fight in Dogtown

I had no idea what the headline meant. I just wanted to get an idea of what era the little boy was from. It was likely that he had died on this day in 1917 and the newspaper he carried was the last thing he remembered from his old life. How a ghost from New York City got all the way out here, I'll never know. He must have followed family out this far or had his soul tied to an object that made its way here.

At Asylum, ghosts were used as messengers. This little boy did not disappoint. "Sirs, the director would like for you to keep and unusually high guard at this time. Someone has broken into Alpha Seven."

The ghost floated toward the locked jail door.

"Wait, kid!" I reached my arm through the bars trying to grab the kid to stop him. My fingers slipped through his shoulder.

He didn't turn around until the lower half of his body was thrust through the steel door. "Yes, miss?"

189

"Did they take anything?" I was panting. I had to know if Baht and Alexander had been freed from their sarcophagus prison.

"Unsure, miss. That wasn't part of the director's message." The little boy completed his transition through the door.

I should have fought my way out instead of coming down here willingly. At the time, I hadn't wanted to hurt any of the strike team guys. They had racked up enough losses lately. I didn't want to add to their misery. Now, I was reconsidering. I *had* to know what was going on.

Marshall, a werewolf with a penchant for chocolate cupcakes, sidled up to my cell. He stared at me while he finished the last bite of some type of baked good.

"If you promise to be good and not get crazy on me, I promise to find out what happened and report it back to you. You've got to give me some time though. I'm not sure anyone really knows what happened yet." Marshall brushed some crumbs off his shirt and leaned against the bars of my cell.

"Fine. For now." I sulked over to the cot in my cell and laid down.

It had been a long ass day.

Chapter 26

I don't know how long I laid in my cell with my eyes closed trying to stop the memories that had been taking over my mind and body since I recovered them in the graveyard. I only opened my eyes because I could smell garlic bread. Someone was trying to torment me. Fitting given the torment I had dished out recently. I lifted my head looking over my feet at Sheriff Larry. He held up a plastic bag from *Gone Fishin'* which was my favorite restaurant in town to get catfish and garlic bread. Most people eat fish with hushpuppies because they don't know garlic bread is really where it's at if you want to bring out the flavor of your fried fish.

"Come and get it while it's still hot." Larry pulled a chair over to my cell and sat down.

I walked over to the visitor's side of my bars and sat on the floor in front of Larry. He passed a can of soda and a Styrofoam box through a break in the bars. I hadn't realized how hungry I was until I opened the box inhaling the combination of fried fish grease and pickles. I didn't care how I looked to anyone anymore. I started shoveling food in my mouth barely tasting it before I swallowed. Larry watched me the entire time I ate. I didn't stop until I caught myself wetting my fingers with saliva so I could eat the crumbs of fried breading littering the bottom of the box.

"Selene," Larry started. Something in his eyes told me he couldn't continue living this way.

"I know." I had no choice except to continue living this way.

"It's just that I'm- well, I'm disappointed and rightly so." Larry kicked back in his chair so it tipped balancing on its back legs.

"I know." I couldn't reply with anything else.

There was a time in my life when Larry being disappointed in me would have devastated me. He was the only father figure I had ever known. Now, given what I truly was, his disappointment was unfounded and unnecessary. I wasn't worthy of such caring. I wasn't used to such caring either.

I had been taught by my mother at a young age that as a woman I had to do things people wouldn't like and those things would ensure my survival. I was taught that hurting other people to get what I wanted was okay because I was royalty. I was worth their suffering, their sacrifice. My mother had tried to sacrifice my happiness for her own when she told me I had to marry Alexander. I had done the same thing to Baht when I killed her without true cause. To an extent, I had stolen Alexander's happiness too when I had killed Baht. I was getting what I deserved. Larry's disappointment didn't faze me. I wasn't the same person I had been yesterday. Maybe if I was still her, I would be more upset.

I got up from my perch on the floor and laid back in my bed. I propped my hands behind my head so I could comfortably stare at the ceiling.

Larry reached through the bars to clean up my mess. His hands were too big to fit through the spaces between the bars. He was able to get most of the trash, having to leave some that was out of his reach. He carefully put the remnants of my old life into the same plastic bag he had taken it out of, tying the handles to seal the bag. Larry stood there for a minute. I couldn't tell if he wanted to say more to me or if he was waiting for me to say something more. I closed my eyes not willing to break the silence with the placating lies Larry wanted to hear about how everyone was right and this wasn't me. This was the me I have always been. If they would have known me at all they would have realized this a long time ago.

I heard Larry sigh deeply before shuffling out of the prison area. Moments later I heard shuffling from another set of feet. His

192

footfalls didn't sound any different in combat boots today than they had in sandals an age ago. Adam was here to complete the band of disappointed ghosts from my past who were trying to teach me lessons I didn't want to learn.

Part of me wanted to see his face, to feel his skin against mine, to taste him. I knew the decisions I had made earlier today made it so I would never be able to do that again. I told myself I made the decision to let him go because I loved him. In reality, I made the decision to let him go because I was selfish and spoiled. I made the decision because I knew he would never agree with me, because he would try to stop me from doing what needed to be done. It was for this reason that I rolled onto my side and faced the concrete wall of my prison cell instead of ogling him.

"I know you aren't sleeping. I know you better than you know yourself. Remember that, always." Adam paused. I didn't turn toward him to see why. "You don't have to look at me. I just wanted to tell you that your spell didn't work. I never once forgot who you were even if you did. You say you got your memories back. I think you're still missing some. If you do what I think you are planning on doing just know that when you leave here I will make it my mission to hunt you until the end of our days. I can't let you go. You are my eternity." Adam's voice choked at the end of his speech. I heard him take a deep breath then clear his throat.

Tears stained my pillowcase as I heard Adam's footfalls get further away until I couldn't hear them anymore. James, Larry and Adam had come to tell me they were with me, they would help me, and I pushed each one away in ways I knew would hurt them enough to get them to not try again.

The tears stopped as footfalls grew closer. All of the people in my life had already been disappointed by me today. I sat up to see who was left that I was forgetting. Reginald stood patiently by the door to my cell. I don't think he knew any other way to stand. I wiped my nose on my shirt sleeve and walked over to him. He dropped a piece of paper on the floor. I bent down to reach through the bars to see what was important enough Reggie would risk the wrath of his boss.

Cleopatra stole the souls of Alexander and Baht.
193

I knew my mother was behind this weirdness somehow. I can't believe she stole Baht and Alexander's souls. What was she going to do with them? I stood up looking at the spot where Reggie had just been. Anubis stood before me wearing the tweed suit Reggie had been wearing. Anubis grabbed my hand through the bars of my self-made prison crumpling the note he had left for me. A sharp intake of breath shot pain up my side. My shirt felt damp. I looked down finding only blood. Anubis was pulling his onyx dagger from my side. When he let go of my hand, my body fell to the concrete of my cell floor. I clutched the scrap of paper to my chest unable to breathe without it. I closed my eyes. Maybe dying here after everything I had done wouldn't be so bad. If I died though, no one would know where my mother was. She had to be stopped. She was the reason I was in this prison.

"Anubis," My voice sounded like shouting to me. I knew I was only whispering.

Anubis used an antique brass key, its head shaped like a scarab, to unlock the door to my cell. He knelt beside me holding my hand. He stayed so silent I thought I was hallucinating his presence. I had watched him dissolve while we were in the Underworld. What if he wasn't here and it was really Reginald? Why would Reggie stab me? He always seemed like a nice old man. He always seemed like he was the only person on Earth who didn't have a bone to pick with me. It didn't matter at this point. Someone had to know. Someone had to stop her.

"Anubis," I swallowed, my bile bitter and metallic. It was harder to breathe now. It felt like the dagger had punctured a lung. My chest felt heavy like it was filling with a warm liquid that could only be blood. I had to tell him. I had figured out my mother's plan.

"Cleopatra is alive. She's going to *Eternal Life*." I coughed a little agitating the moving liquid in my lungs, "my father..." I didn't wait to see his reaction. I didn't wait to see if he would do what I asked of him. I closed my eyes letting myself fall into the waiting abyss.

Memories that had been returned to me but still forgotten plagued my dreams making it hard to rest even though I was sleeping.

Chapter 27

When I woke up I confirmed my worst fears— my memories would never be of unicorns and rainbows only darkness and death. And pain. And fear.

The light was too bright. I couldn't see where I was going. Maybe I wasn't really going anywhere. The Earth felt like it had stopped spinning which was good because I had a splitting headache that was making me nauseous. I closed my eyes making the world turn once more.

Something plastic gripped my arm as I stirred trying to roll onto my side. The plastic was a warm hand wrapped in a rubber glove pinning my upper arm to a cold flat thing that I was laying on. A shiver traveled up my naked back. The convulsing my body started without my permission slid the sheet that had been covering me onto the floor. I had been here before. I had to stop this from happening again.

All of the energy I had previously wasted trying to keep myself from vomiting was now being redirected to fighting whoever was holding me down. I would not be party to another autopsy performed on me without my permission. I tried to sit up. I managed to get halfway propped up on my left elbow before the stranger's hands pushed me back.

"Stop moving, Selene. They won't believe you're dead if you don't play your part."

The voice of my latest murderer sounded muffled. He must have had on a face mask. If I was naked on a metal slab and Anubis had on gloves and a face mask pretending to be something he was not, I must be in the morgue at Vampireville. How did he know if he stabbed me I would come back? I didn't even know that if I died again I would come back. I thought it was Baht's soul keeping me alive all this time. If not her, then what? Would I ever get to end my miserable existence?

Have I mentioned lately how much I hate magic and all of its bullshit rules? Well, I do. Now you know. Something inside of me was screaming that this death would not be my consequence for using the *Book of the Dead* one too many times. I couldn't wait to see what the universe had in store for me. First, I had to break out of Vampireville. It would be much easier now that I wasn't in a prison of my own making.

I willed my mind to calm my body. Anubis was right. If they thought I had survived death without Baht's soul helping me I would get thrown back into vampire jail. Sure, it was all my fault that I was even there in the first place. Right, I had pushed away my entire support system. Yes, I needed to get over myself. There are a lot of things in life I know but never acknowledge I know. If I did everything everyone expected of me then I would never have time to do the things I loved like... Okay, so maybe I needed to take some time for retrospection. First, I really needed to get out of this morgue and into some warm clothes.

I was too involved in myself to notice Anubis had covered my naked body with the sheet that had fallen during my fit of panic.

"Selene, I can get us out of here if you trust me." Anubis's voice was still muffled.

I guess since everyone thought he was dead too he felt the need to hide. If anyone found out he was alive he would be welcomed with a parade. The only way I was getting a parade now was if the whole of Vampireville lined up to throw stones at me as the strike team marched me back to vampire jail.

"What do we do?" I tried to whisper without really moving my mouth. I didn't know who was around. Since most of the people in Vampireville had amazing hearing, word travelled fast. I didn't want my words to travel faster than my getaway would take.

"Enjoy the ride." I could hear Anubis smirk behind the surgical mask he wore.

Anubis covered my head with the fold of the sheet. I closed my eyes and tried to enjoy the ride like he said but Anubis was a terrible gurney driver. He kept bumping into walls and pushing me full throttle over the bumps of door jams. I was getting nauseous again. Every so often Anubis would say hello to someone. How were we not getting caught?

After a steep incline I was jostled some more while Anubis loaded the gurney, presumably onto a truck because I wasn't fitting in the backseat of a car like this. My whole body shook when Anubis slammed two doors. I heard a creak of a hinge and felt another shudder jolt through my body as he opened and closed another door. A diesel engine purred to life. We were moving. I hesitated for a split second before sliding the sheet off my face.

There were cabinets full of medical supplies on either side of me and a short row of oxygen tanks strapped to the opposite wall. How on Earth had Anubis waltzed me out of the front door of Vampireville into a waiting ambulance without anyone trying to stop him? I covered myself with the sheet moving gingerly toward the cab of the truck. Anubis wasn't there. Reggie was driving the ambulance.

I startled and tried to back up at the same time Reggie hit the brakes for a red light. I only succeeded in tripping and tangling myself in the sheet. Anubis had betrayed me. I was exposed. Reggie had always been kind to me. He was also James's right hand man. The only thing he was capable of at this point was turning me in to the guards at vampire jail.

I folded the sheet in half before wrapping it around me again. This time I tied it in several places which fashioned the sheet into a sort of mini-dress toga like I used to rock back in the day in Egypt. If Reggie noticed that I had risen from my crypt and was no longer laying on the gurney, he didn't say anything. I took a quick glance out of the windshield to see where we were. It looked like we were on Highway 31 heading south to Birmingham. Away from Vampireville was the opposite direction I thought we would be headed. I dropped the scalpel I was gripping back into the open supply drawer to my right.

I climbed into the passenger seat. Reggie gave me a nod without taking his eyes off the road.

"Reggie-" I started to ask him what he was doing here. He cut me off.

"Reggie? What?" Reggie looked at his face in the review mirror and frowned.

Reggie's body trembled slightly during his transformation into Anubis. He looked in the rearview mirror again and nodded his head now satisfied with his appearance. I wasn't as satisfied. I wanted to know what the hell was going on. No better way to find out than to ask. With blunt force as was my custom.

"What the hell is going on?" I was shouting. Great, I was back to normal.

Anubis smiled. I guess he was as happy as I was that I was myself again.

"I disguise myself as Reginald when I don't want anyone to notice me or question what I am doing."

"I was wondering how you got me out of Vampireville without having to kill anyone. Well, other than me."

We were quiet while I looked out the passenger window at the scenery. There wasn't much to see. Black and white cows dotted the landscape breaking up the muted greens of the trees and grass.

"Anubis," I turned towards him in my seat, "I watched you die in the Underworld. How did you come back?"

Anubis sighed. "With Lord Osiris missing from the Underworld, souls have been escaping their fates. I escaped my fate as well. There was too much to do here to leave you alone, mistress."

Anubis concentrated on the road ahead. We were almost passed the cut off to go to the site of my tomb. I sat up a little straighter, craning my head, ready to watch the road to my eventual fate pass me by. If I didn't meet my mother at *Eternal Life* tonight, I would catch up with her eventually. I was enjoying my time with my friend. I didn't want to ruin that by stopping the potential end of the world. I sighed. I couldn't watch the world burn at her feet. I had to stop her. I was just going to tell Anubis to go to my tomb when out of the corner of my eye I saw a truck approach the ambulance from behind.

Instead of passing us on the left like a normal person, the pick-up rammed us. Anubis and I pitched forward. Our seatbelts were the only thing keeping us in the cab of the ambulance. Anubis recovered before I did and hit the gas. The ambulance accelerated inches away from the pick-up's bumper letting us go a few more feet without being rammed again. The reprieve allowed me time to remove my seatbelt and make my way to the back. I flung open the back doors of the ambulance ready to throw one of the liberated oxygen tanks at the truck once it was close enough.

I should never have looked at the vehicle's driver. Or, you know, put the heavy ass tank down before hesitating to throw it like I did. Adam was driving the pick-up that was trying to run us off the road. I couldn't hold the tank above my head any longer. I dropped the tank letting it roll out of the back of the ambulance. Adam watched the tank fall swerving at the last minute to avoid a collision. The oxygen tank bounced on the cracked pavement before rolling to the grass peppered gravel shoulder.

Adam told me he would find me if I ever left him. I thought I would have more time. I thought we would all have more time. Of all of the things I thought I could fix in my life, my relationship with my husband was not one of them, not after everything I'd done. I steadied myself to throw the last oxygen tank at Adam's truck. The timing was right. Adam's truck was lined up perfectly behind the ambulance. I let him get close enough to lock eyes with me. I couldn't let myself fall for his gaze this time. I threw the oxygen tank at the same time he rammed the ambulance with his truck.

I didn't see Adam crash. I only heard his tires screech while I looked up at the ceiling of the ambulance from the flat of my back. The crash had thrown me backward into the ambulance. When the ambulance stopped spinning I crawled toward Anubis. He was slumped over the steering wheel. I could smell blood. I pulled myself up by the driver's side armrest.

Anubis was still breathing. He would be fine. I'm pretty sure he's survived worse. We both had which is why I didn't let worry about what to do next paralyze me and steal my consciousness. A quick glance at the passenger mirror confirmed what I already knew to be true- Adam was on the wild hunt and I was his prey.

I unbuckled Anubis's seatbelt and pulled him from the driver seat. I took his place. Dammit. My feet couldn't reach the pedals. I heard the truck door slam. Adam was on the move. All of that panic I had been holding back flooded my brain. I was frantic in all of my movements now. I felt around under the driver seat for some kind of lever to pull the seat forward. The crunch of gravel under Adam's heavy footfalls combined with my own labored breathes created a combustible situation that played out in my mind more times than I cared to count. Adam's crunchy footfalls stooped. He paused, listening to something we both heard in the distance.

Sirens. Shit. Forget pulling the seat forward. I would just stand up to drive. Winging it had been my M.O. since before I was born. I would figure something out. I would survive Adam's love for me. I would survive my mother. I could do this.

I turned the engine over and closed my eyes as I hit the gas. The ambulance lurched forward slow at first. I opened my eyes when I felt the ambulance pick up speed. I'm glad I did. I almost ran us into one of the lone guardrails littering the side of the road at random and unhelpful intervals. I righted the ambulance at the right time. I checked the driver's side mirror since I couldn't see the rearview mirror well. No one was coming that I could see. Things were finally looking up.

The ambulance shuddered. My foot slipped off the gas causing the ambulance to slow. Did Adam ram us again? I put my foot on the gas chancing a glance from a full body twist to the swinging back doors to see if Adam was behind us. No one was there and the ambulance was slowing down again even with my foot pressed all the way down on the accelerator. Facing forward again I saw the reason. The fuel and check engine lights had come on along with some other lights warning me to maintain my vehicle sooner rather than later. I took my foot off of the accelerator. It didn't matter what I did now. This metal box on wheels wasn't going anywhere else for a good long while. I let the ambulance roll to the shoulder. I didn't bother turning off the engine. It just sort of took one last shuddering breath before it died on me.

I knew Adam wouldn't be far behind. I squeezed out from behind the steering wheel trying not to step on Anubis's prone form as I made my way to the back of the ambulance. There had to be something I could use as a weapon. I remembered the scalpel I put back earlier. I reached for the drawer and screamed. Someone grabbed my leg. I shook the clammy hand off and jumped on the gurney.

"Shit, Anubis!" I screamed at my only friend in the world while he laughed his ass off. "We don't have time for this shit. Adam is on his way and so are the cops who work for Vampireville." I hissed through my clenched jaw.

Anubis steeled himself. He used his sleeve to wipe mostly dried blood from the side of his face. "How do you know they work for Vampireville?"

"Maybe they don't. Things can only get worse from here and having a bunch of humans who don't know who we are, what we are, will only make things worse." I hissed back.

Anubis stood up. "Did we stop because we crashed? How bad is it?"

"While you *napped*, we crashed, were almost caught by Adam and I drove the ambulance until it no longer ran." I jumped off the gurney and went back to rummaging.

202

Anubis paced the ambulance in two steps. He looked out of the back doors making his concerned face. I turned back to the ambulance supplies. A door slammed. I was still mid-air from the unexpected noise when the second ambulance door slammed shut. I shook off my bad feeling vibes. I didn't have time to die right now. Anubis moved the gurney so it blocked the back doors. He grabbed the chain that had been supporting the oxygen tanks I had relieved us of earlier. He looped the chain around the gurney and door handles marrying them together in unholy matrimony to some chemicals he had carefully placed in a container without mixing.

The sirens got closer. Cops were coming. Adam probably wasn't far behind if he wasn't the one leading them right to us.

"Selene, I have to tell you something about your father." Anubis grabbed me by the shoulders looking so far into my eyes the blackness of my soul shrank against his touch.

I could feel him, all of him. He was of the Underworld. He was from the only place I had ever belonged.

I shrugged Anubis off. "Tell me later."

"There might not be a later. Listen," Anubis stopped me from crawling into the driver seat. "Selene, Osiris is your father."

I just stared at him. I mean I never knew my dad anyway. He died when I was a baby. It wasn't all that far-fetched that Osiris could be my dad. Why the big reveal? Why now? Did anyone else want to vomit at this current moment in time? Just me? Okay, then.

"Your parentage is the reason why you cannot die even with Baht's soul removed from your body. It's the reason you have survived having a second soul this long. I'm afraid even the blood of your father won't keep your soul from tainting for eternity. I'm even more afraid that the process has already begun." Anubis looked like a kicked puppy.

I reached out to ruffle his hair. He looked like I was going to slap him. I pulled my hand back biting my lip. Everything Anubis was saying made perfect sense. The sirens, so close my ears felt like they would bleed at any moment, and the slamming car doors stopped me from telling Anubis that he was right. My soul was almost full dark with no hope of light on the horizon.

"Get in the front. When the back doors blow run to the nearest car and take off. Don't worry about me. We'll meet again in the Afterlife." Anubis kissed the top of my head pushing me into the driver seat. He was putting himself between me and the anticipated explosion.

Run.

I had to get ready to run.

I had to leave my only friend in this world to die again.

I couldn't watch him die again.

I swore this time I wouldn't let him die for me.

Here I was breaking my promises.

I was always breaking my promises.

Chapter 28

I was out of the driver's side door a split second before the back of the ambulance erupted in a blaze of glory. The force of the explosion pitched me forward. I hadn't expected whatever Anubis put in those containers to create such a mess.

I heard a woman scream. I put my hand to my mouth to check and see if it was me. It wasn't. I was pretty sure Anubis didn't scream and if he did it wouldn't sound like a fashion model with her hair on fire. I wanted to get in the police car and drive away but my conscious finally got the best of me. I couldn't keep living my life the way I had been. I couldn't keep pretending I didn't care when I really did.

I didn't know how to get back into the inferno I had just escaped in a way that would allow me to cheat death a second time in as many minutes. Where the ambulance used to be was now a wall of flames licking at the clouds in the sky like they were made of ice cream. I paced the space between where the ambulance should have been and the police car for a half a second. I couldn't think with the police siren screeching like a pterodactyl flying headfirst into a volcano. I got into the driver's seat of the police car and pressed buttons on the center counsel until the lights and sirens shut off. I had one foot out the door when something hit the windshield with enough force to create a million tiny cracks throughout the glass.

I jumped out to see what happened. Anubis's prone body was draped across the windshield of the police car like he had just decided to lounge there and take a nap. I saw movement out of the corner of my eye. It wasn't Adam chasing us.

"Mother, how good to see you again." I shouted above the flames heating my face. My insides were heated with white hot rage. The fire did nothing to squelch that.

"Selene, my dear, sweet baby girl. Have you changed your mind about joining me?" Cleopatra was unfazed by the flames lapping at her heels.

"Maybe. One question though, is Osiris my father?" I wanted to see if Anubis's intel was right. Maybe I could find Osiris and ask him for help. I wondered if my mother ever loved Osiris or if she just wanted to use him like she wanted to use me. I wondered if Alexander knew who our father was or if she kept him in the dark just as much as me.

"No, not him. What does that matter now? Osiris is dead. I killed him. I'm sure you saw that the Underworld was unguarded on your last little jaunt down there." Cleopatra looked smug.

I guess killing a god made you feel important. Really, all it made her was a dick.

"What's your game, mom? To take over the entire Underworld? Why? There is nothing there." I was trying to thread something together with mismatched pieces and missing information in my mind. I knew her plan. It was on the tip of my tongue.

"Darling, you are my plan. You have been since before your birth." Cleopatra smiled making me shudder.

She stomped her heavy boot on the pavement. Instead of the skin tight police uniform she had been wearing, she now had on skin tight, barely there traditional Egyptian garb. I was seeing way more of my mother than I ever wanted to know existed. She had a staff with a forked end and the head of a cobra on top. A small medallion of the closed Eye of Horus had been tied to the staff in the middle with a leather thong. The staff looked royal and ceremonial. I had only seen one other person wield such a thing.

206

The ground shook. It was hard to notice at first. Anubis's Eye of Horus necklace bounced up and down on his bare chest. He had turned back into his true form. You know, the mostly naked guy with the wolf head. Yeah, he was a total hottie even with a wolf head. The fact that I thought he was hot even in death was so me. Good to know that being stupid when it comes to hot guys didn't go away if the guy was dead.

The faster the ground shook the more fissures appeared in the pavement. The ground didn't stop shaking until the fissures were large enough for demons and hellhounds to crawl through. Which they did. Without Osiris keeping order in the Underworld, the things that haunt the night came out to play. So did some guy who looked exactly like James's brother. They both had easy smiles and sandy hair. Trouble was, this guy was hiding some real evil shit behind his smile. He was the guy from the other side of the coin with my mother's face I had been keeping in my pocket. I patted my right leg absentmindedly. I didn't have the coin on me to confirm it was him. It must still be at the Vampireville morgue in the pocket of my jeans.

Set, the god of chaos stood before me. He also happened to be the owner of the staff my mom was holding, which he took back from her when he completed his ascension from the Underworld. Set looked a little worse for wear like he had been imprisoned for a good part of the past two millennia. Made sense as to why he wasn't around for my formative years considering he was my father and all.

Anubis had been wrong. Osiris wasn't my father. His brother, Set, god of chaos was. My mother's plan was to con Set into fathering her children so those children would rule for eternity as pharaohs made possible only by their status as demi-gods (the children of gods and mortals). I have apparently been the worst daughter who ever existed and the best at ruining all of my mother's plans since birth. First, I was born a girl. Second, I refused to marry my brother because I was in love with Adam. Third, I wouldn't die like I was supposed to. I've been a real bitch that way. And I know exactly where I get *that* from.

Now, here I was ruining my mother's life yet again. I didn't have time to worry about the past or whether or not Adam was alive. I could still feel him. Despite my treachery, our souls would be entwined for eternity. Anubis clench his fist. Good. I was wondering when his lazy ass would get up. Better for him to get up angry and prepared to fight.

The part of my mother's plan I had been struggling to figure out finally took shape in my mind. "You stole Alexander and Baht's souls to trade them for Set's, didn't you?"

My mother never misses an opportunity to gloat. "It was too easy breaking into Asylum to get their souls. Thank you, darling, for leaving their souls gift wrapped for me."

At least we knew Alexander wasn't the one who broke them out and that he and Baht were out of play for this little party. Anubis stirred. I hoped he was ready. It was now or never.

I took my chance. "Mother, father, prepare yourselves to be sent back to the Underworld. For good this time."

What stood between me and a fighting chance at killing my parents were about a thousand demons and hellhounds. Oh, and the fact that my parents were gods and no one told me. Yeah, that. I took a deep breath. This was going to be fun.

"Who is going to send us back to hell, child, you?" Set laughed barking like a seal with laryngitis.

My father didn't even know my name. Great. I was a little over two millennia old and he hadn't even bothered to learn my name while he was in prison. I was so *not* getting him a card next Father's Day.

Set stood tall using his staff and my mother's shoulder to keep himself upright. He was injured. Maybe I did have a fighting chance after all.

"I will, brother." I didn't have to turn around to know James stood behind me. Or, rather, Osiris since they were one in the same.

That must have been what Anubis was waiting for. He took the opportunity of his master's triumphant return to get his ass in gear. Anubis jumped off the hood of the police car with the ease and grace of a cat trained as an acrobat. Yes, I do know that seems redundant to say since cats are pretty graceful and acrobatic already. If you would have seen him, you would have agreed.

I turned to welcome Osiris with my patent what-the-hell look when I saw Adam standing beside him. My heart skipped a beat. Told you I still felt him near me. Osiris and Adam joined Anubis by my side. My mother looked like she was going to have a cow right there amidst all of the inky shadows she thought she commanded. Set rolled his eyes. Apparently epic battles was something these brothers did every millennia or so to blow off steam. Even in his weakened state he seemed to think he could beat Osiris.

The demons and hellhounds knew better. Some of them receded back into the fissures that bridged this world to the Underworld. Some of them slunk off into the shadows filtering onto the pavement from the setting sun through the trees lining the highway. Those that stayed looked like they didn't want to. I guess they thought it would be worse for them if they left and Set actually won this time. Maybe it would have. IF Set was actually going to win this time.

I looked at the boys. We all knew Set belonged to Osiris. I had to call my sparring partner before someone else took her.

"Cleopatra is mine." I didn't wait for the boys to acknowledge my decision.

I walked through the throngs of demons and hellhounds to stand before my mother. They let me pass without disturbing me. That should have been my first clue that something was up. I was too hyper-focused on killing my own parents to realize I shouldn't have been able to wade a path through demons and hellhounds so easily.

My father laughed. My mother tried to plunge a dagger in my heart. At the last split-second before my mother would have succeeded in killing me I lunged for her. As I tackled her to the ground, she stabbed me in the shoulder. I punched her in the face.

Remember how I said earlier that I had an aversion to pain and suffering, especially when it came to my own pain and suffering? Yeah, getting stabbed in the shoulder hurts and I was pissed. I guess it was a good thing since I was such a shitty fighter. I fully believe a thousand percent that anger makes you a better fighter.

My mom tossed me off of her like a wet rag in the sink. I bounced off the still smoldering ambulance left-overs onto the shoulder. My mom and I wiped the blood from the corners of our mouths with the backs of our hands at the same time. I guess that cleared up one thing- I wasn't adopted.

I checked the progress of the boys. Osiris and Set were grappling hand to hand like wrestlers. It was actually kind of comical since they were gods and should have been leveling each other with the magic in their pinky fingers.

Anubis and Adam were fighting the demon hoard. They were both skilled fighters. It was still hard to watch. Adam was under a hellhound using his bare hands to keep the hound's jaws from snapping shut on his neck. Anubis side swept a demon's legs out from under it. After he stabbed the demon with his onyx blade, he went to the hellhound on top of Adam thrusting so intensely into the hellhound's back he hit the heart. Adam coughed twice and got up with the aid of Anubis's hand. They briefly patted each other on the back like the brothers they should have been born to be before they folded themselves once more into the fray.

Sirens leveled the heavy breathing in my ears. I hadn't realized I was panting so hard until I couldn't hear my breath anymore. Sheriff Larry and some of his deputies jumped out of their cruisers to fight the demons and hellhounds. Osiris stomped his left foot on the ground sending magic toward Larry and his deputies. Once the purple magic reached them, they all transformed into werewolves sans full moon. None of them stopped to panic. The amped up their attacks now that they had teeth and claws to fight with.

I turned my attentions back to my mother. I caught her off guard with my stare. She had been watching Set and Osiris battle for the grace of the Underworld. It was a little unsettling to see the concern my mother had for my father. She had never shown this side of herself to me before.

Breathe.

In.

Out.

Good.

Your mom is not capable of love. She is evil incarnate and must be killed. Got it? Yes. Okay. Do your duty to your people and stop this monster before she hurts anyone else.

I picked up a piece of jagged edged ambulance. I tossed it back and forth in my hands for a second. Then, I charged my mother pushing her to the ground, using my weight on top of her to drive the metal piece into her stomach. When we were horizontal she coughed. Crimson splashes of blood sputtered onto my face.

"Adam, look out!"

I looked up to see Anubis fighting to get to Adam. Every demon he killed was replaced by two more. Anubis was too late. A demon's hand glinted silver as the last rays of the sun sank behind the horizon leaving us in a perfect darkness, a darkness we all belonged to.

Adam was too still. I could feel him leaving me. I didn't want to be alone on this Earth without him. He was my eternity. His soul belonged to me and mine to him.

"No!" I screamed.

My mother took that opportunity to drive her knee into my side. I doubled over. She pushed me off of her and jumped up. Adam was dead. I knew I should want to fight my mother to stop her from hurting anyone else like she had been hurting me for so long. I just didn't have the drive to fight. I didn't have the will to live knowing Adam was in the Underworld without me.

"Even if you join him, he will never love you again after what you have done." Cleopatra stood over me. Oddly enough, she wasn't smirking. She didn't want to be right about this even though she knew she was.

211

Her dark eyes bore into mine. She offered me her hand. There was something about the gesture that seemed maternal. I couldn't remember a time she had ever looked at me like that. I lost all reason and took her hand. She pulled me close to her with her right hand. My heart was touched by the gesture of love. My brain knew better. It just didn't warn me until after my mother's left hand stabbed me in the stomach with the same shard of ambulance I had stabbed her with a few moments ago.

"Mom?" My right hand gripped her shoulder while my left travelled from my stomach to her face. I touched her cheek letting my hand run down the side of her face to her mouth in a red scream before dropping to my side.

I should have expected her to stab me in the back, or the stomach. I wanted to fall for her beautiful lies one last time.

Cleopatra dropped my body. I turned my head to watch her hobble over to where my father fought. Set was doubled over in pain. Osiris didn't have a scratch on him. Something tugged my arm. I jumped a little. I had been too busy watching my parents struggle to stay alive to see Anubis join my side.

"Selene, get up. You are better than this." Anubis pulled me into a sitting position.

I fought him to lie back down.

"Adam told me something before he died. He wanted me to tell you if he didn't make it through this battle that he was sorry and he still loved you." Anubis bent down to throw my body over his shoulder.

He wasn't going to let me die here tonight despite the fact that it was my turn and I wanted to. I groaned. Anubis set me down concerned he was exacerbating my wound. I stood on my own breathing heavily. My wound was worse than the wound my mother sported. I was in way worse shape. I rested my head on Anubis's shoulder. The pavement was slick with blood. Crimson and black swirled together in a mesmerizing pattern. The black blood reminded me that Anubis had been fighting hellhounds and demons. Why did he stop?

I struggled to lift my head. There were no more demons or hellhounds to fight. Most of Larry's men were still alive. There were a handful of griffins flying around with demons clutched in their talons. When had they gotten here? There was Osiris and Set battling while my mother watched and Adam's corpse lying lonely and cold in the middle of where the battlefield used to be.

"What happened to all of the demons?" A little blood trickled out of the corner of my mouth.

Anubis used his sleeve to wipe the blood from my face. "After Adam fell, the number of demons increased. Larry and his men were dropping off in the heat of battle. Most of them had never battled a demon before. If Reginald hadn't come with the griffins, we never would have dispatched them."

"Reginald? I thought you *were* Reggie?" My head was swimming with too much information to process.

"No, I was never Reginald. I used to dress like him to gain access to places I wouldn't normally have access to." Anubis was pushing me off his shoulder.

Nap time was over. I looked over at the battle my mother was witnessing. She stood clutching her stomach, watching my father get up from the ground again and again while Osiris pummeled him back down each time.

"Are you tired of this yet, brother?" Osiris stepped on Set's hand preventing Set from grabbing his staff.

Set spit blood on Osiris's feet but would not relent. Set tried to get up. Cleopatra shuffled over to help him up. "Not now, woman."

My mother stopped where she was. She fought back tears. Maybe she did love my father after all. Too bad he didn't seem to love her.

I slipped Anubis's onyx dagger from his belt. I ripped a piece from his tunic that was already frayed and tied it around my hand and the dagger. I didn't think I could hold the dagger on my own. My grip, along with the rest of me, was failing.

"Selene, you don't have to do this. Osiris will stop them both." Anubis grabbed my elbow.

I registered a couple of griffins covered in thick black demon blood stretched out on the pavement. They were too far away for me to be able to tell if they were alive or not.

"I know."

I pulled away from him walking steadily toward my mother, stepping over the bodies of men I once knew.

I faltered with my foot raised when I saw the face of the man I was about to step over. Larry was lying on the ground not moving. There were blood and claw marks marring his naked body. He had turned back into his human form. I stooped to check his pulse. He was dead.

"Mother!" I screamed my battle cry finding enough resolve to rush her.

She didn't look away from the fight. As I got closer, I could hear labored breathing that rivaled my own. I spun Cleopatra by her shoulder to face me. She knew what I meant to do. My mother took one last look at my father coughing blood onto the pavement with Osiris standing over him with his foot on Set's back holding him down.

"I'm ready." My mother whispered letting the only tear I had ever seen her shed fall from her eyes.

"Me too." I whispered back.

I drove the onyx dagger into her chest. Her body didn't fall to the ground until I pulled the dagger from her heart and drove it in my own.

Epilogue

The road to hell was still paved with living skeletons. That was the only thing that stayed the same since my last trip to the Underworld. Osiris's return restored the balance between the living and the dead that kept the natural order of things in check. The sky was brighter, the gates were all open, the three-headed monster was back to being a happy puppy and souls were milling about free to roam without consequence. Some were in line waiting to be judged and sent to their final resting place. Some were standing before a wall painted with the symbol for Ra, the sun god, debating on asking Ra to take their souls back to the world of the living and sprinkle them into the wind so they could be reincarnated.

It was a far cry from the dreary landscape I had witnessed before. Even the souls trapped inside of the skeletons I was currently standing on top of were quiet. Their eyes, still as whole as if they were alive, no longer pleaded for grace and mercy. They knew why they were being punished this way and accepted the consequence for their actions.

At the end of skeleton road, Reggie stood in full griffin form hitting Larry with his tail absentmindedly. Larry broke into a grin when he saw me. I couldn't help smiling back even though I knew they were all dead. I waved, happy to see the only people in the Underworld I considered friends.

Anubis stood hand in hand with Ammut. It was good to see them both again despite Ammut trying to kill me the last time I saw

216

her. I had a feeling if I met anyone else from my past here in the Afterlife, they would have tried to kill me or I would have tried to kill them. That was sort of how my life worked when I was alive. I hoped things would be different now. I also hoped that if I were to be judged and sent to live amongst the skeletons that now carried my weight, I would be as at peace with that punishment as these souls seemed to be.

I walked up the path towards my friends careful not to step on any faces. For a brief moment I considered what it would feel like if I were to step on one of the whole eyeballs protruding from the eye sockets of the skeletons. I shuddered letting my imagination run wild for a minute before reigning in my thoughts. I was finally at peace with what I had done in life, finally worthy of death. My soul felt lighter than ever. I didn't want to start back with my bad habits so soon.

Anubis hugged me. Ammut was more reserved. She seemed embarrassed by what she had done. I wasn't going to spend my afterlife ashamed. I hugged her. Her body stiffened before she was able to relax and hug me back. Larry clapped me on the back. It still felt like he had his werewolf strength even in the Afterlife. Reggie nodded at me as was his custom.

"Where is Adam?" I asked slightly breathless at the possibility of seeing him again, of spending the rest of my Afterlife making it up to him.

"That is for later. Now is for your judgement. I am honored to ferry your soul to its eternal resting place, mistress." Anubis bowed low to the ground. Ammut followed his lead.

I looked down noticing for the first time the meadow I was now walking on. The scenery in the Afterlife had changed without me detecting what was happening. I was walking on the same grass I trudged through on my last trip. This time, the color of the grass was more vibrant, the blades softer and the dirt underneath holding the earth and grass together was not full mud holding me in place. I breathed in clean, fresh air. The entirety of the Underworld was in Technicolor in sight and smell. This was my new happy place.

Anubis led us to a cabin on the outskirts of the field of souls where I had found Victor. I hovered at the edge of the porch. The cabin looked like the one Alexander had taken me to.

Anubis came down the cabin steps to take my hand. "My Lady, please come this way."

I wrenched my hand from his. I was in my own version of hell. I knew I didn't deserve this much peace. I had done too many things in life to blacken my soul. This was wrong. This was all wrong. I backed up further bumping into Ammut. Her frown told me she had no clue why I was freaking out and she was over my bullshit already.

"My Lady?" Anubis didn't try to come any closer. He just held his hand out waiting for me to take it.

My panic attack started. I couldn't breathe. I had to get my shit together one last time. I wasn't going to let this be my ending. This would not be my eternity.

Osiris came out of the cabin. "Selene, this way." Osiris waved me up the stairs.

I was still reluctant. I knew Osiris was fair and would not send me to eternal damnation at the hands of my brother.

Adam was sitting by the fire when I walked in. I quickened my pace stopping short when I realized he might not be as happy to see me as I was him.

"Selene, Adam, I have a job for you." Osiris didn't care about my love life or about the fact that I was dead for good this time.

Once a dick, always a dick.

Neither Adam nor I jumped at the chance to work for Osiris. He didn't care if we wanted to work for him or not. We were doing it.

"I need you to walk between this world and the world of the living to help Anubis ferry souls to their rightful places. I also need you to track lost and escaped souls. Drag them back to the Underworld if you have to. Anubis will provide you with everything you need.

Good luck." Osiris didn't wait for questions. He left the cabin with as much fanfare as he had when he revealed he was Osiris and not James.

Anubis and Ammut followed Osiris leaving me alone with Adam. I had no clue what to say to him. I didn't know how to apologize for what I had done. I didn't know if he still wanted me as much as I wanted him. It didn't matter that his dying breath had been to tell me he still loved me. A dying man's words could be trusted only slightly more than the words of a used car salesman.

"Adam, I-" I stopped when I felt Adam's hands ruffling my hair from behind.

His lips didn't leave mine for a long time. It was a good thing neither of us needed to breathe right now. When he was satiated by my undying love for him, he broke away from me.

Adam stood beside me holding out his hand.

"If you have eternity, so do I."

96205915R00124

Made in the USA
Columbia, SC
25 May 2018